The World Beaters

OTHER BOOKS BY ED KLEIMAN

The Immortals (NeWest, 1980)
A New-Found Ecstasy (NeWest, 1988)

The World Beaters

Ed Kleiman

© 1998, Ed Kleiman
All rights reserved

No part of this publication may be reproduced or transmitted in any form or by any means, graphic, electronic or mechanical, including photocopying, recording, or any information storage and retrieval system, without permission in writing from the publisher. Requests for photocopying of any part of this book shall be directed in writing to CanCopy, 6 Adelaide Street East, Suite 900, Toronto, Ontario, M5C 1H6.

Canadian Cataloguing in Publication Data

Kleiman, Ed, 1932 –

The world beaters

ISBN 1-895449-80-4

1. Title.

PS8571.L396 W67 1998   C813'.54   C98-920174-0
PR9199.3.K47 W67 1998

Book and cover design by J. Forrie
Art Direction A.M. Forrie
Typeset by Thistledown Press Ltd.
Cover photo by Ellen Moffat

Printed and bound in Canada by
Veilleux Impression à Demande
Boucherville, Quebec

Thistledown Press Ltd.
633 Main Street
Saskatoon, Saskatchewan
S7H 0J8

The Canada Council | Le Conseil des Arts
for the Arts | du Canada
since 1957 | depuis 1957

Thistledown Press gratefully acknowledges the financial assistance of the Canada Council for the Arts, the Saskatchewan Arts Board, and the Government of Canada through the Book Publishing Industry Development Program for its publishing program.

CONTENTS

The Wedding I Never Attended
9

The Day the Messiah Came
27

The Getaway Car
47

How the Free Trade Act Nearly Ruined My Cousin's Bar Mitzvah
68

A Memorial for Johnny
93

Lucifer in Starlight
114

The Hallelujah Girls
133

The Ruined Garden
150

The World Beaters
184

"Forgive Me, Father, for I Have Sinned," She Said
202

The Annunciation of Love
223

ACKNOWLEDGEMENTS

The following stories appeared in the publications listed below:
"A Memorial for Johnny" – *NeWest Review*
"The Day the Messiah Came" – *Short Story International* (under the title "The Romantic")
"The Wedding I Never Attended" – *NeWest Review* and *Under NeWest Eyes: Stories from NeWest Review* (Thistledown Press, 1996)
"The Hallelujah Girls" – *Prairie Fire*

The author gratefully acknowledges receipt of a travel grant from the Manitoba Arts Council to research one of the stories.

Characters and events in this collection are fictitious. Any resemblance to persons living or dead is purely coincidental.

*For my mother, Luba Kleiman, with love
And in loving memory of my father,
William ("Bill") Kleiman (1901 - 1984)*

The Wedding I Never Attended

Some people like to learn about the future by having their palms read or their tea leaves deciphered. Some like examining the entrails of slaughtered enemies. I prefer wedding photos. They seem to me foolproof.

My brother Barry's wedding took place in Lethbridge, back in 1957, and I've always regretted not having attended. Not that I'm overly fond of such functions. Too often they're dominated by a sense of duty that just leaves me feeling dull and tired. You must come and smile and stay, whether you like it or not. But what I see in the photograph I have of my brother's wedding — all those impossible people collected together at that impossible event — is what has totally vanquished the fates that, till then, had held sway over our family from Day One.

Marriages in our family have always been revealing events. My parents' matchmaker was the Russian Revolution. An extraordinary claim? Not really. My mother's family lived in an immense two-storey house in the south end of a village called Balta — near the Black Sea — and my father's family lived in little more than a hovel in the north end of that same village. With the coming of the

Revolution, a radical redistribution of wealth took place, with the local Red commissars pocketing everything that hadn't been hidden away. The hovel was used to house Red cavalrymen, and my father's family was billeted in the second floor of my mother's home. So my father and mother met.

"I didn't even know he existed before the Revolution," my mother says with a note of astonishment still in her voice. "Then one day they moved in upstairs as if they'd always been part of our family. And not just one person — my future mother- and father-in-law, their sons and daughters, and a son-in-law as well."

"It was a surprise, for sure," my father says. "But later when the Bolsheviks had us marching through the village with wooden rifles, I knew it was time for our family to leave. I would send for your mother later. The next day we were gone."

"With all *our* sheets," my mother adds testily.

"We needed them for crossing the Prut River into Roumania."

"You *flew* on them, I suppose, across the water like on a magic carpet?"

"No, no. You forget. The river was covered with ice and snow, and we crawled across under the sheets so the border guards could not see us."

"And *we* had to sleep on bare mattresses," my mother concludes.

Three years later, after my father's family had fled Roumania and set sail for the Canadian prairies, my mother's long-held hopes were fulfilled when she received a letter one day, all the way from Winnipeg, proposing marriage — along with a Cunard ticket for the next boat to leave Riga.

There they all are, in Barry's wedding photo, my father in a tuxedo and bowler hat, neither of which he's ever worn again, and my mother in a long dark evening gown that tells you, in no uncertain terms, that despite the lack of sleeves or even shoulders it cost a bit. But the clothes don't fool you for a minute. You look into those faces and you see the Russian Revolution there, the toughness, the determination to escape. The photographer and guests and lavish wedding hall are barely acknowledged: tolerated, yes, but just for the moment.

To the right of my mother is her niece, Anna, with her husband, Mel. The faintly tragic air on Anna's face as she gazes at the groom is all that is left of the adolescent crush she'd held for my brother, a passion long ago forgotten by most people, but one which still means a lot to my mother Rose. She still sees Anna as Barry's best friend and, accordingly, *her* best friend. As a result, she would, without hesitation, do anything for Anna, except maybe dying — and would probably do that too, though she'd have to think about it for half a day first.

Anna is enormous, over two hundred pounds. Her elaborate hairdo, combed high and fluffed out, makes her look even bigger than she is. Her dress is specially made, blue taffeta over silk, and costs more than anyone there would earn in a month. On her right hand she wears a clear blue sapphire, simply cut, that flashes out its unmistakable message for a circumference of at least thirty feet: *Money! Money! Money!* Her necklace and earrings are no less opulent. The face she turns to the world is childlike, open, radiant. In my mother's eyes, Anna would be a goddess if she weren't such a scandal. All that passion combined with all that weight and jewellery leaves my mother puzzled.

But Anna isn't puzzled. The weight she sees as part of the Buchalter curse of clumsiness and awkwardness. Downright doltishness. She's heard it in her father's voice, that bumbling quality; whereas from her mother she gets her expensive tastes, style, critical eye, intelligence, wit. But at times they threaten to disappear, almost totally submerged in her huge frame. Anna is a battleground between grace and oafishness, and she looks upon her predicament with no small degree of amusement. Also, it is a challenge which she dares not ignore.

Anna's mother does not care for this particular son-in-law, and she is not at all bashful about letting everyone know it. She will not tolerate his calling her "Mom." And so, much to her annoyance, he has taken to calling her "Fanny".

"Well, Fanny," he says as both families gather after the wedding rehearsal — one of the many events in Lethbridge described to me later — "You've got to admit, no matter what you thought of me before, that I've provided your daughter with everything a wife could hope for: a house, car, money, children . . . "

Impatiently she cuts him off. "I don't have to admit anything." Her eyes still flash with anger even though Anna and Mel were married almost ten years ago.

"But what else could Anna want?"

The anger rises in her voice. "A husband the world could respect!"

Once more Mel senses defeat, though not yet its magnitude. He knows his reply sounds apologetic so he makes the words boom out. "Well, Anna likes me well enough."

"That *naar?* — that fool?" Fanny translates just in case he doesn't understand, "she never did have much taste." And she glowers at Mel, acknowledging him to be the living proof of her statement.

Mel is more gigantic than his wife. His mother-in-law holds even his size against him. *Even?* I should say *especially.* He sells women's underwear in Miami (another sore point), and his store there is the most successful in the whole city.

When I think of them flying all that way from Florida, I envision the plane just barely able to skim the treetops. In Lethbridge, they rent the biggest, poshest car available: a purple Lincoln convertible. Everyone in town knows the car. Hertz uses it mainly as a promotional model in TV ads, but there it is suddenly on the streets of Lethbridge and in it two *superhuman* beings.

Everything in Lethbridge becomes smaller in their presence. "Isn't there a bigger hotel?" Mel asks as he enters the lobby of the Marquis — Lethbridge's best. "A better restaurant?" "Larger stores?" Mel's voice booms through the streets and my mother Rose looks at him proudly, telling everyone that he is her nephew and he owns the largest and most successful store in women's underwear in Miami.

Mel became intensely interested in that line of clothing when he was still a high school student and discovered that he had grown to such huge dimensions that his mother was forced to make his undershorts. Certainly, no underwear sized XXXL was available in the stores. And he later discovered that what was, as an adolescent, the source of both embarrassment and awe had become a lifelong passion. Underwear. But no signs of all that pent-up, teenage lechery now remain. Nor of his adolescent recklessness.

For weeks in grade ten, St. John's High School had been abuzz over what had happened one Sunday afternoon. When his best friend's parents, the Schellenbergs, were out at a YMHA meeting, Mel and a few friends had actually been able to convince some bold and adventurous girls to play strip poker in the Schellenberg's garage. After three frenetic and sweat-stained hours, the girls had emerged, red-faced and triumphant, not only still wearing all their clothing, but also in possession of Mel's trousers, shirt and extra-large underwear. Wearing an oversize woman's raincoat — taken from the closet of his friend's mother — Mel had had to flee home over backyard fences and narrow back alleys.

But now no one would ever have guessed at his earlier embarrassment. He looks about him at waiters, gas pump attendants, policemen — in fact, at everyone in Lethbridge — as if he could buy the City Hall and the whole town itself and raze the whole mess to the ground if the town insisted any longer on annoying him with its smallness. "Why, a fellow could walk around this whole town in just a morning," he says. "Provided he didn't walk too fast."

But Anna knows how to keep his outrageous talk in check. Words never fail her in any crisis, and that gift has served her, as well as her mother, very well. In Miami she's become editor of the sales catalogues for women's clothing stores, and, in minutes, she can put a discrete-but-telling paragraph down beside the most outrageous

— and transparent — article of clothing. For Mel her strategy is simple. "Just don't forget," she scolds, "who taught you how to play poker!"

But if Anna has, throughout the years, been my brother's secret admirer, then my Aunt Faigele, my father's only surviving sister, has been his outright nemesis. Between my Aunt Faigele and Barry there are no devious strategies employed, no cunning slights or equivocal phrases. Between them it is outright war.

The day has long since passed when my aunt could forgive the things he's said about her. When she'd phone our place and was unlucky enough to get my brother Barry on the line, he'd announce loudly, "Well, if it isn't Cuckoo Bird on the phone!" And then, turning to us, "Anyone want to speak to Cuckoo Bird?"

"Barry, don't be such a pest!" my mother would scream. But just let my Aunt Faigele say anything even slightly critical, and my mother prepares for a scorched-earth campaign.

Aunt Faigele is thought of as cuckoo by most of the family. Not because of what she is, but because of what she does. She's always wanted to be a millionaire, you see, and if only she could have scraped together a little more capital, with her initiative and enterprise, she'd have made the Reichmans take to the hills long before the banks forced them to. She buys and sells properties, rents out apartment blocks, opens second-hand stores, bids on condemned buildings, runs a neighbourhood newspaper, has opened a bakery, started up a Jewish theatre in a cinema that folded, and has plans, eventually, first to take over the North End and then the whole city of Winnipeg — all with resources that total no more than five hundred dollars. How? By mortgaging properties she doesn't quite own yet, then getting bank loans using those properties as collateral, and later moving swiftly and expertly into stocks and bonds whose volatility would frighten off even the Rothschilds. She has at times emerged from business deals owning whole blocks of the North End. Once I heard her trying to explain just one part of such an arrangement when she was outlining to my father why he should again bail her out of trouble with the banks.

"Don't be such a pussycat, Velvel," she cried. "What's five thousand dollars when next week we can have forty thousand?"

"But Faigele . . . "

"Velvel, I'm so disappointed. What would our mother say? With your money to invest, I could be a millionaire already five times over."

The only trouble was that her business arrangements were so intricate that no one, not even she, could for long retain a firm grasp of all their complexities. And she didn't dare write them down for fear they could become evidence if she were ever tried for tax evasion. So when she forgets all the ins and outs of a business deal and all speculations collapse like a house of cards, and the banks foreclose and the bailiffs come, and the tax collectors send letters, she has only one recourse. She has a nervous breakdown. And the rest of the family has to tidy up the mess as best it can.

But Barry's jibes draw vehement attacks from her as well. When my mother announced, as so many North End mothers announced right after their son's bar mitzvah, that he would one day be a doctor, Aunt Faigele attacked at once.

"You see this arm?" she cried out, pushing back the sleeve of her blouse. There the arm was: puffy, shapeless, an unhealthy white. "When grass grows on that arm, then your son will be a doctor."

But she's still not buried in the earth, and Barry is a doctor and she looks from the wedding photograph with astonishment on her face. She was determined to come to the wedding, to see for herself the bride and her family. She hadn't really believed in their existence. For that matter, she didn't believe in Lethbridge's existence. So she said to her husband, Morris, "Tell your boss, there in the CPR station, that next month we go to Lethbridge."

"But, Faigele, it's not yet my vacation time."

"Vacation time, schmacation time. Tell him."

"But how will we afford the clothes? The trip?"

"You just tell him for a week to find someone else to sweep the floors in the station. The clothes and the trip and the hotel I'll look after."

And she is as good as her word. Clothing departments at Eaton's she had never before visited were suddenly startled into an awareness of her existence, *transfixed*, you might say, and it would be months before they recovered from the shock. An evening dress, pearls, handbag, coat, shoes — the most expensive, the most stylish — in her they all encountered a challenge their designer had never dreamt of.

"But how will we pay?" Morris cried in astonishment that night.

"Who's to say we'll pay? Tell me, did I say we'd pay? Eaton's is Eaton's and Faigele is Faigele." And then Morris understood.

The train journey to Lethbridge was harder to arrange, as there were no trains arriving early in the morning and Faigele was determined she would not miss anything on Barry's wedding day. But there was an early freight from Calgary, and although Morris's railway pass alone might not ordinarily have got them into the caboose of that train, Faigele's presence at once vanquished all opposition. So it was in the caboose of the morning freight that they arrived in Lethbridge. And then it was on to the town's major hotel, *The Marquis*, to camp on the floor of a relative's rented room. The hotel did not long survive the aftereffects of that visit. Before many years passed, it was torn down and replaced by the Royal Bank Building, which ever since has gazed warily toward the railway station for any signs of yet another freight train bringing newcomers to the town.

Aunt Faigele is more lavishly dressed than anyone in the wedding picture — except possibly for her husband, Morris, who looks both uncomfortable and amused in his brand-new tuxedo. Perhaps that is because all the sales tags of his clothing have been folded in. They tickle his neck and stick uncomfortably into his waist, though they don't appear in the photo. But Faigele doesn't look uncomfortable. She's used to wearing clothing with the price tags still on. She doesn't even notice them anymore. And if the powers that be at Eaton's ever intend to have any more of her business, they better get used to having most of her purchases returned.

She feels no qualms at all about returning clothing to Eaton's. After all, thirty years before she'd returned her wedding dress. "What!" she'd said in astonishment, "to wear it one time and pay such a price? I have a better idea." And if she would return *that* item of sentiment and memory, she will return anything.

Why, several years after her marriage had taken place and she'd gotten into the habit of returning everything she'd worn only a day or two, she'd adopted a brother and sister ten and eleven years old. Having her own children had been made impossible two years earlier because of the complications of a miscarriage. Adopted, did I say? Well, sort of. *Bought*, as a matter of fact, and smuggled across the American border. Our family is used to getting smuggled across borders. Three hundred dollars apiece, they had cost her. And a bargain at that. Or so she had initially thought.

I still remember the whole family being brought over to meet these new relatives: two blond children with hard faces looking suspiciously at all the adults dressed as if for a celebration. But they didn't last three weeks. Children, for Faigele, required just too much patience. They had reacted blindly — breaking some of her best dishes, stealing her watch and cutting up the new sweater she'd meant to return to Eaton's. So back across the border once again those children went. Not for her to cope with juvenile delinquents. It's true, there were no price tags to pin back on them, but still she got most of her money back. I sometimes think of those two — the blond brother and sister. They should have been in the wedding photo as well. How foolish for them to have created such a ruckus during those crucial first few weeks of their adoption. If only they'd been more accepting, Aunt Faigele would have made sure they survived, that they became successes. With her, they could have thrived.

So buying clothes she would later return to Eaton's and getting onto the caboose of a freight train and camping on the floor of a relative's hotel room hardly strained Aunt Faigele's nerves at all. She and Morris, in their still-to-be-returned clothing, stand to the left of my mother and stare out at the proceedings, she with astonishment that this impossible event should be occuring at all, and he with that puzzled look of amusement on his face, which — on second glance — looks to be more at this new display of her daring than at anything else.

Before they leave, in a passenger train this time, she will try to buy the hotel they are staying at and for years afterward will complain that her new Lethbridge relatives should not have intervened when the deal was all but salted away.

Now, at last, we turn to the bride and groom. Of Brenda, I can say little. She was a stranger to me then, and at first I see only a proud figure in white staring steadily into the camera. But is there even then, behind that look, a quality to her smile that reveals such surprise at this outlandish family she's married into?

My brother Barry is easier to describe. Perhaps. The face is dark and downcast. All the pain of the last ten years is there for everyone to see, but they do not recognize it. His troubles began with an IQ test in Junior High School that revealed — to everyone's astonishment — that he was brighter than anyone who'd ever taken such a test there before. That test was a curse. It made him arrogant — impossible to tolerate. The teachers giving the test had agreed not to reveal the results to their pupils, but like everyone in the history of the world who has ever administered such tests, they blabbed out all the results within seconds of tabulating them.

The effects were, in some ways, disastrous, though no amount of arrogance could blunt his interests. Those were the days when he read John Dos Passos' *U.S.A.* and couldn't find anybody but me to discuss the book's experimental nature with. And what did I know? Nothing. The book got him interested in jazz, cinematic techniques, architecture, sociology, aeronautics, astronomy, even grinding lenses for a telescope he was making.

"Look at what he's doing with the book here," he insisted. "He's using newspaper headlines in fiction. And jazz in his sentences."

"So?" I said dumbly.

Then he'd turn to the piano and play some passage from a Duke Ellington piece. "Can't you hear the same music in this paragraph?"

"What music? Which paragraph?"

But my brother's real problems began when he passed into Grade Ten and all his newfound arrogance caught up with him. There he was mocked for all his interests, spoken of as pretentious, became the butt of teachers' jokes. And so he quit school in the middle of winter and nearly destroyed us all.

What's worse, he fought back with the wrong weapons. He became pompous, conceited, a namedropper. In fact, he became the stupidest person with the IQ of a genius that I've ever met.

A low point came when I was home for weeks with a broken ankle, the result of a missed vault in gym class. My brother, who was reading a book on the chess masters, offered to play a game with me.

"I'm going to win this game," he announced, "without your taking any piece higher than a pawn."

"Let's just play."

"And if you win more than three pawns, I'll buy you a dinner at Wally's Steak Loft."

We played for hours all afternoon and into the evening, each move taking as long as half an hour. Again and again, we each worked out the consequences of the game to its conclusion. The game itself went on for three days — with my mother screaming in alarm and my father storming out of the house in disgust.

On the fourth day, I struggled on crutches with my brother to Wally's Steak Loft. "But the food isn't even kosher!" my mother screamed down the street after us.

Wally's Steak Loft was a flyblown place with wooden benches. We were served by a surly high school dropout who saw in my brother someone giving himself airs, someone who was in reality no different than himself.

At the end of that meal, which tasted like *dreck* — just plain old shit — my brother asked, "Now tell me, Michael, tell me, did you ever taste a better steak?"

This to his younger brother who Barry knew had never tasted steak before in his life. "Thanks a lot, Barry," I lied, and after he left a dollar tip for the contemptuous waiter, I limped out with my brother at my side. That night, after everyone had gone to sleep, I threw the chess game into the garbage.

But just when all seemed lost and beyond the point of recall, he began taking evening classes and correspondence lessons to finish high school, and then he went on to university. His grades got him through Medicine, but his pompous manner undercut his every achievement.

Knowing the results of that high school IQ test has cost him pain every day of his life.

But who is the bride, Brenda, who has seen beyond the pompous tones and arrogant manner? I see her leading him out of that high school as if out of a tomb.

So the wedding for Barry is a rebirth, and his mother, standing so stalwartly beside him, is transfixed by a kind of ecstasy as he emerges at last into the light. Fleeing the Russian Revolution and setting sail for Canada has been a minor triumph compared to this. Cousin Anna, behind her in the photo, knew all along what was there, but no one would listen. And then perhaps there were times when even she doubted what her teenage infatuation had revealed to her astonished eyes. It *was* an infatuation, she knows. Besides, cousins don't marry cousins anymore. But still she is pleased to have someone else share her vision of Barry.

Of course, Aunt Faigele sees only the devil who called her "Cuckoo Bird" on the phone. She *knows* this marriage will never last. Barry's pompousness, she is sure, will once more make him a figure of ridicule. So why should she pay real money for clothes to attend an unreal event? The sales tags pinching into her body are a constant reassurance and comfort that not one penny will be lost. She gazes at my brother Barry and his bride as if they are a mirage.

The look would shake even me if it weren't for the radiance in Brenda's eyes, for whom this wedding, despite all obstacles, had become the most real event of her life.

I gaze now at other faces in the wedding photo. At Brenda's parents. Who is to say what is in those faces? The mother wears a hat that scandalizes our family for years afterwards: a bright yellow and brown thing that would look more appropriate on a farm at the height of the harvest.

Who are they, these new relatives? Brenda's father is a clothing manufacturer who turned out thousands of military uniforms in the last war. But his is not a warrior's face. It is round and gentle. He wears glasses which do not quite conceal some pain in his eyes. I look from face to face and then pause at Brenda's younger brother, Mortie — that smart-aleck look. Yes, here is the source, I am sure.

Brenda's mother is looking at Anna with astonishment. That immense stone on Anna's finger, that gigantic hairdo. She'd be patronizing if she didn't recognize there a native taste and sense of style that is beyond her understanding. She has never before met anyone of Anna's size and obvious physical strength, and they make her aware of her own frailty: the lines on her face, the fragile lightness of her body. Anna's healthy face reveals nothing but her openness and good humour, yet Brenda's mother is just beginning to suspect how ridiculous her hat would look in Anna's eyes.

For Anna is too goodhearted to patronize anyone. Besides, on this trip from Miami, in fact this very morning, Mel was unable to get out of bed, couldn't even see for a couple of minutes, though his eyes were wide open. She can remember only too well the symptoms preceding her father's final stroke for her not to guess what the future holds in store for them. So she stands there aware of Mel's bulk — and her own — and of how all their intelligence and wit must struggle against the oafish giants they have become.

The Wedding I Never Attended

There are grandparents as well, and aunts and uncles, cousins, nieces and nephews: locked-in faces, faces with suppressed rage, faces that radiate a single note of innocence like a struck tuning fork, proud arrogant faces whose good looks will never become beautiful. They are all there, new in-laws as well as old relatives — a curious family — some governed by powerful fates for far too long, recorded with photographic clarity, yet not all that easy to read. There is my family that I'm getting to know better with each second that I gaze at this photo. Do I sense my mother's perseverance in some yet unknown in-law? Or my aunt's darkness in a new cousin I have yet to meet? I gaze at this photo as if at members of a family I've known all my life. I blink and the next moment they are strangers. Yet there was one fleeting moment when I glimpsed their fates.

Have you not glimpsed that moment also? Do you not know this family? and I yours? this larger family at a wedding you and I have never attended? I see them all before me: the groom, the childhood sweetheart, the dark suspicious aunt, the father in a tuxedo, bowler hat and dark polished shoes that he was forced by his wife to buy. And the bride — the radiant stranger entering into our lives, wearing a gown from which all sales tags have been carefully snipped because she fully intends — despite all tradition — to be dressed in this gown once more before leaving this earth. That knowledge serves as a dark background from which she emerges in white. It serves, as well, as a centre of strength for the whole photo.

Though my new bride and I could not be at Brenda and Barry's wedding, for we were on *our* honeymoon (a brief European tour in between two years of teaching in London), I have always been glad that we were able, in the midst of busy Venice, to find a glass-blowing factory where we could buy their wedding gift: six red wine glasses with golden rims and a decanter, red as the wine it was meant to contain. A wish from the Old World following them to the New, smuggled in with the clink of glasses touching and the unspoken words of greeting, vanquishing forever the land of bitter memories — of Wally's Steak Loft and the struggles of our youth.

The Day the Messiah Came

"Don't make me a grandfather!" I heard my cousin shout just as we got out of the elevator. His younger daughter, Debbie, had been married that afternoon to Ronnie Finkleman — a North End boy if there ever was one. The wedding reception was being held on the seventh floor of the Fort Garry Hotel.

"I'm too young to be a grandfather," Sheldon explained to my mother as he poured himself another shot of rye.

"You? You're fifty years old. It's time."

"I like driving my Jaguar at racing meets in Toronto and Minneapolis. I like visiting the tables in Las Vegas. I like sailing off to the Virgin Islands in the middle of January."

"The Virgin Islands? You're looking *there* now for virgins? You've given up finding any around here? With the company you keep, you could look far and wide and still not find any. You have to give up such childish games."

"Auntie Rose, I'm not even used to being a father yet."

"Don't listen to him, Debbie. He's a fool, your father. He wants to go on running to the gambling tables with other women and he's breaking your mother's heart. He's fifty years old and still he hasn't grown up.

"For you, Debbie," my mother plunged recklessly on, "for you I promise, before all these people, to your first baby I will give a big present."

A present?

"What kind of present?" asked Sheldon.

About us, heads were turning. Relatives drew closer.

"A present?" their faces asked.

"Of a thousand dollars. Make him a grandfather, Debbie, so he can't break your mother's heart with other women. Make an end to his running to the gambling tables and to those islands. The Virgin Islands yet — the big fool!"

"It's time I found Ronnie," Debbie announced uneasily. And then happily glancing beyond my mother to us: "Hi, Michael. Hi, Christine. Glad you could come."

"She's probably already pregnant," Sheldon said in a voice that carried beyond the small group.

"Be still, fool!" my mother shrieked.

Up to this point, Debbie had looked quite elegant, but now her face was flushed a vivid red as she strode from the hall and made toward the banquet room entrance. Blocking her way, though, was my Uncle Harry, who was talking to some business friends. They were dressed in tuxedos, with heavy five-o'clock shadow to match, all dyed-in-the-wool North Enders. Their trousers kept drooping low on their hips, ties were askew, and cigars or hand-rolled cigarettes glowed crimson with each puff. Uncle Harry is about seventy-five, wears glasses and a hearing aid, but he's as quick as ever in smelling out a good business deal. In one hand he held a shot of rye and in the other a particularly obnoxious cigar. The group had just burst into laughter, if not over Sheldon's outrageous comment, then over the folly of some business rival, when Debbie, determined to escape her father's teasing, passed by in full stride. At that precise moment, Uncle Harry stepped backward — smack onto the train of Debbie's wedding dress, his scuffed, unpolished black shoe planted firmly on the white-lace filigree! She lunged forward as the dress suddenly tightened about her body. The dress tugged so at her shoulders that her arms started to slip out of the sleeves, and the front of her dress was dragged downward until her momentum was abruptly halted. As she turned furiously towards the arresting force, the top half of her white filmy brassiere was revealed, followed by just a hint of the pale twin moons that were her silky breasts, about to make their premature début on the spot.

Uncle Harry let the cigar drop from his nicotine-stained fingers so that it landed within a fraction of an inch of all her lace and filigree. Debbie came that close to emerging naked from a fiery blaze. The sight — even to Harry's jaded senses — made his eyes widen. Then he stepped off the train of her dress, and Debbie fell forward into the banquet hall.

"You see," said Sheldon. "She's too young to get married. She should have waited."

"When you grow up, Sheldon," said my mother, as we made our way toward the banquet tables, "when you're no longer a little boy, you'll be as big a fool as your Uncle Harry there."

Just then Debbie's mother, Rhonda, came storming up to us. "What has Sheldon been saying? I can just imagine that husband of mine. Don't listen to a word."

"I was saying how wild I still am about you." Sheldon could not be shamed.

"Since yesterday, you mean?"

"So tell me, you two," asked my mother, staring shortsightedly at the numbers on the tables — and determined to prevent Sheldon and Rhonda from quarreling on their daughter's wedding night — "the little numbers are for what, Rhonda? Which one tells where I am sitting?"

"Where else should you sit, Aunt Rose, but at the head table with us? And, Michael, you and Christine are to sit at the table with my in-laws, Jake and Sidney, and their wives. They're at the table nearest the window. Look at the seating plan."

"Well, at least we can look out the window when we run out of things to say."

"Stop it, Michael," whispered Christine, "you'll soon be as bad as Sheldon."

The seating was another one of my cousin's practical jokes, I thought, as Jake and Sidney carried on about grain deals in South America they were in the process of concluding. But just as I was wondering if rather than simply looking out the window I should jump out of it instead, Jake stopped quoting the stock market and leaned toward Christine.

"Rhonda tells me you and Michael are going to New York for a few weeks."

"Yes, beginning the first of the month — providing we can find a place to stay that we can afford."

"Oh, that's not difficult."

Impressed, I took another look at Jake: dark hair swept back to one side, moustache, pearl-grey suit, pink shirt and white tie. His voice was soft and deep.

"I know some people who own a hotel at Rockaway Beach. The weekly rates are very reasonable. It may sound light years away from downtown Manhattan, but there's a train that will take you into Grand Central Station in no more than half an hour."

"That would be perfect. Grand Central's not far at all from the New York Public Library."

"Consider it done, then. I'll phone Howie tomorrow to let him know you're coming."

"Jake, I hope you'll forgive me for asking," Christine said, "but I just can't place you in Michael's large family. And here you've even offered to do us this big favour. Just how are we related? I should know, but I so rarely see you. Just at the occasional bar mitzvah and wedding — like now."

"I'm Sophie's son."

Trust Christine. So straightforward. Clears up the confusion that even I had struggled with forever. Of course, Jake is Sophie's son. Sophie is my cousin Sheldon's older sister. But when I looked at Jake again, why did that seem so difficult to believe? Easy. Sophie was so awkward, so bumbling, and her voice had a gravelly quality that's quite unusual in a woman. Yet Jake looked — and sounded — like one of the princes of the world: sauve, self-possessed, informed.

"I kind of get the feeling, Jake, that you could have found us accommodation at such short notice anywhere in the world," said Christine.

"He probably could have," volunteered his brother Sidney.

"How come?" I asked.

"Well, Jake's a sales agent for a Winnipeg grain firm — Goldberg's. During the last sixteen years, he's travelled just about everywhere."

It seemed that he'd only recently come back from Rio de Janeiro, where he'd made large sales of rye and oats. And in two weeks he'd be flying to London to negotiate an even larger contract for canola and cereal grains. Then he'd be stopping in New York to meet representatives of the American government who wanted to engage in discussions about how trade allotments involving third world countries could be consigned in a way that would best benefit American and Canadian suppliers.

"In all his travels," said his wife Edith, "he always finds some reason to go back to New York. Isn't that right, Jake?"

"That isn't fair," said Sidney. "You've no right to speak to him like that."

"I have every right."

Edith was short and plump with dark hair. Early thirties, I would have guessed. Her face wore a tired, almost cynical air, the sort of look that had simply grown tired of questioning the credibility of what Jake was saying. Her overall appearance was plain, pedestrian, the sort of person you would never notice in a crowd. By contrast, Jake stood out.

After dinner, while we were dancing, Christine said, "I think he's the most charming of your relatives. In some ways, the most charming person I've ever met."

"In what ways?" I asked, momentarily losing the beat of the music.

"In *all* ways," she replied.

"I think I'll jump out that window after all."

"I can see that most women would be just overwhelmed by him. In fact, *I* am overwhelmed."

"So why does his wife look that way?"

We both looked over at Jake, on the dance floor now with one of the bridesmaids, a pretty blonde. He was whispering something into her ear, and just to look at her glowing there, you could see it had nothing to do with grain sales. At the dinner table, Edith was clearly worried as she talked to her sister-in-law Anne, who seemed to be trying to reassure her.

"Now, I know what you're thinking, Michael..." Christine laughed.

"I haven't said a word."

"You're just jealous."

"You bet I am," I teased. "London, New York, Rio de Janeiro. Why, he wouldn't even have to snap his fingers, and there'd be pretty girls galore."

Later in the evening, I saw Jake dancing wih his wife, Edith, and she too was glowing, though not with pleasure. "Go, then!" I heard her hiss as they danced by, "go back to that New York apartment. See if I care. But this time, Jake, *you* can explain to the children."

More fierce words were exchanged until she stormed out of the banquet room, just narrowly missing getting torched by Uncle Harry, whose lit cigar was once more gesturing wildly as he explained to his cronies how he had hoodwinked yet another business rival.

That night, while driving my mother home, I asked about Jake Spector. "He's a decent boy. And Edith is a fine wife. And his children are gold and silver — such beautiful children."

"Oh, Mom," said Christine, "I knew I could count on you." And then turning to me: "Aren't you ashamed to be so suspicious of Jake? Your mother knows the whole North End, and if there were anything — any gossip — about Jake, she'd know it."

We were now passing by the City Hall and were in a seedy area of town where drunks gathered in threatening groups outside beer parlors. "But Jake, he has his problems."

"Jake doesn't look like the kind to be held up by problems, Mom."

"These ones, no one can solve."

"What kind of problems?"

"Heart-attack problems. A few years ago he nearly died. For weeks, he lay in the hospital — not alive, but not dead either."

"And he still travels? Makes business deals?"

"His wife begs him to stop. His mother Sophie screams, if he doesn't stop, she too will have a heart attack. Goldberg says he'd go even himself and let Jake look after the office. Every day he is away, they prepare to sit *shivah*. But Jake won't listen. Even as a boy he would never listen. Just like the rest of the family. But a hero, also — not for him to be a cripple. And yet, for sure, a fool he is, too."

I sank into gloom as we drove beneath the CPR subway and headed towards West Kildonan. "Sorry I said a word."

"You should be. And when he phones tomorrow or the next day about a place for us in New York, I want you to really show your appreciation."

Several choice responses came to mind, but rather than face years of recrimination later, I remained silent.

"He is getting for you a room in New York?" asked my mother. "Why?"

"Because Michael and I have some research to do at the New York Public Library. You remember we told you before we'd be going there for a month. We'll be getting back just before classes at the University begin."

"So?"

"What do you mean, 'So?'"

"So he knows in New York many people. He will be in New York at the same time, his mother tells me."

"Yes," said Christine. "He mentioned that he's always negotiating grain deals with other countries. He's been everywhere."

"Everywhere?" I asked.

"Yes. In France, Brazil, even in Egypt, he's been."

"In Egypt?" We both started. "Isn't that dangerous?"

"In the time of Sadat, Egypt needed grain, and you know that big shot Goldberg — such a businessman — he's scared of no one, not even Sadat. He would have gone himself, but Jake said, no, he would go. Always, he'd wanted to see the pyramids and the sphinx."

"And?"

"So he saw."

"Wasn't he scared?" asked Christine.

"Scared he should have been. But not Jake. For weeks, Goldberg heard nothing. His wife, Edith, his mother, Sophie — they heard nothing."

"He should never have gone."

"For sure. But go talk to him. Stubborn like a mule."

"But he did get back," interposed Christine.

"Yes, one day another trader at Goldberg's, Izzy Ackerman, phoned from New York — from Rockaway Beach. They all stay by the same hotel in New York. Jake was there."

"Thank God! What a relief that must have been," said Christine.

"Some relief. He was there with a girl."

"You're joking."

"You think I'm joking? Some joke. A girl — from Egypt yet."

"From Egypt?"

"A very clever boy Jake is. He went to sell grain and with a girl he comes back from Egypt. Who ever said they were not good bargainers in Egypt. And the girl — like a flower. More beautiful than a dream, Izzy says. Izzy and Jake went together to the same school. Izzy says that, for her, even Solomon would have forgotten all his other wives."

"Sounds to me as if Izzy fell in love, too. But Jake got there first."

"And Jake, he is not Solomon. And this is not the time of Solomon. He already has his own wife, his own children."

"So what happened?"

"At first Goldberg thought two of his best people he'd lost. Not a word he heard for a week after that first phone call. And every day Edith phoned him half a dozen times. Then Goldberg heard Jake had called her — and a few days later he and Izzy were back. Such a scandal it was! The whole North End knew! And every month to New York he'd rush for a few days — and what could Goldberg do?"

We were now into West Kildonan. About us passed by street upon street of a community that was as closely knit as an eastern European village.

"She came all the way from Egypt with him?" asked Christine.

"She is young — still in her twenties — yet she came."

"She left her country and her family for a stranger — just like that? Wasn't it dangerous for her?"

"Of course it was dangerous. Falling in love is always a dangerous proposition. Doesn't matter for who. When I first came to Canada in 1925, I saw then such a boy — so much like Jake, they could have been twin brothers. His name was Alfie Silverman."

The name stirred in my memory, but I couldn't place it.

"Did you never hear of Alfie Silverman?"

"I recall something about a wedding that never took place."

"Ah, that you recall. The wedding was all arranged. The girl came and her family came. Your father and I and other friends of the Silvermans came. But the Silvermans never came and Alfie never came."

"Why?"

"Because they were all fools."

"But why?"

"Because Mr. Silverman was scandalized. His boy had only to stay in Medicine from January to May and he would be finished. But in December he told his parents he wanted to marry a girl he'd met at the Medical Clinic — a nurse."

"And she wasn't any more Jewish than I am," guessed Christine.

"And she wasn't Jewish," my mother confirmed. "But Alfie wouldn't listen. Whatever his father said: 'Wait till next summer at least. Let the family meet her. The two families should have a chance to talk.' Alfie would not listen at all. His father threatened to have a heart attack; his mother went into hysterics. But Alfie was determined."

"So what happened?" asked Christine.

"So his father phoned all Alfie's friends from university," said Mother.

Vague memories of the story came back to me: of an impromptu stag and of Alfie getting blind drunk and then being driven across the US border far into the night.

Wide-eyed, Christine listened as the story unfolded.

"So when he woke up later, he didn't know *where* he was or even what *day* it was."

"But where *was* he?"

"In Las Vegas," I answered. At last the details had come back.

"They took him all the way to Las Vegas?"

"Alfie's father thought it was a good idea."

"And what about the bride?"

"The bride? I saw her by the wedding. So pretty she was. So sweet. When Alfie didn't show up, I thought she would have by herself hysterics or maybe a heart attack."

"But what happened to her?"

"A year later, she found someone else, and this time she sent her father and brother to see that he got to the wedding. Afterwards, they went right away to live in Montreal. He's a real estate agent."

"And Alfie, what happened to him when he sobered up?"

"He became so upset he didn't know what to do. He tried to phone her, but she hung up the phone in his ear. When he phoned again, the father answered, and that was worse."

"So what did he do?"

"He never came back."

"Never came back?"

"He took all the money he needed to finish medical school and he went to New York and bought a ticket for Palestine and till this day he is still there — in Israel."

"Did he never write to her? What became of him there? Is he married?"

"From that day to this, he never writes his parents. A cousin in Haifa wrote me once she heard he became a farmer in a kibbutz."

"And his parents?"

"Such fools. They send letters to relatives there, but from him never a word — after all these years."

Recalling all the details of that event had made her angry all over again. After a brief farewell, she brusquely slammed the door of the car behind her and made her way impatiently up the front path to her house.

The next afternoon, Jake did phone, and afterwards, when Christine came into the living room, she was glowing with the news. "Well, he did come through for us. A place in Rockaway Beach for $150 a week, provided we stay for a minimum of two weeks."

"That's amazing."

"It's miraculous."

"But we still have to see what the place is like."

"Oh, why are you so suspicious — you and your family?"

She's right. Why am I?

I must confess, when we arrived at Rockaway Beach, I was astonished. It was a small hotel only two blocks from the ocean. And when we returned from Manhattan each night, backs stiff from too many hours of making notes in the library, there would be a table reserved for us in the dining room. The weekends we spent swimming or sailing. Any day, I thought, Jake would appear in the hotel lobby, but although we sensed his presence everywhere, he himself remained invisible — as did the mysterious woman who'd followed him to New York from Egypt.

On the late TV news, I took to watching a dark-haired commentator for the PLO who appeared at least twice a week. Her face was radiant, and there was a gentle, delicate quality to her movements that was nothing short of hypnotic. Her words were punctuated with short, awkward pauses that gave an innocent, childlike quality to her statements. The overall effect was that you wanted to help her finish each sentence; you wanted to believe in every claim she made. And I, in my youth, like Jake, had always been a Zionist in my sympathies. What could her effect be on others? There formed in my mind the notion that she was the mysterious creature Jake had met in Egypt and had later left behind in New York. Whether or not this was true, I never did discover during our stay, though on a tour of the UN building I made enquiries, only to be rebuffed by a suspicious information officer.

I did not see Jake again till several weeks after we'd returned to Winnipeg. I had gone to the Pan Am Pool for a swim on a Friday afternoon. University classes had only just begun and the strain I felt at getting back to teaching was expressing itself as a piercing pain in my side. Welcome to age fifty, I told myself. Joy to the world! Still, get in twenty or thirty laps, and all will be well again. Yom Kippur was only one day off and I wanted to start the year with no disturbing quaver sounding through the ram's horn for me.

When I came out of the locker room onto the pool deck, there was Jake rising from the diving board in a way that made the pain in my side ache all the more with envy. He rose effortlessly — like a sunrise — in a pose that seemed to have nothing to do wih the vibrating sound of the diving board behind him, and then jack-knifed and cut sharply into the water. At the pool's side, I waited for him to come up beside me. His arms tensed, braced as he gripped the wet, tiled surface, and then he rose in one quick powerful motion from the water. His appearance at once dismissed all talk of a heart attack as just another North End rumour.

"Good to see you again, Michael. Do you come here often?"

"Not really. I've been meaning to phone to say thanks for that place in New York."

"Yes, Christine said you enjoyed it. I saw her this afternoon as I was coming out of the Grain Exchange. She was going to pick up some tickets at the Theatre Centre. We had coffee at *Bottles*."

"Christine's been asking me all summer to take her there. Did she like it?"

"Seemed to."

"Curious the way these things work out — the two of us seeing you on the same day. I sensed you might be here today. When I came in, I said to myself, 'Jake will be here.' Don't know why. In fact, I had the same feeling when we were in Rockaway Beach. Every time we went for a swim I expected to see you coming out of the water, and now you finally have."

"It would have been a long swim," he laughed. "I've been in Winnipeg all summer. But I'll be going to New York at the end of next week to sew up a grain deal. All that grain will be getting taken off the prairies soon. Has to go somewhere besides a grain elevator."

"Any chance of seeing you before you leave?"

"Christine was suggesting we all get together some evening. Perhaps when I get back from New York."

His words were like a tonic. Whatever suspicion I once had of him had vanished. The pain in my side that could stab upwards towards my lungs and leave me gasping for breath was gone. I dove into the water in an arc designed to leave all aches and pains behind. When I finally came up for air, I looked back to the poolside, but Jake had vanished. I swam thirty laps without cheating — never once pausing for a few extra breaths at either end — and when I left the pool all the excitement of the summer at Rockaway Beach had returned.

When I got home and mentioned seeing Jake, the delight that sprang to Christine's face was instantaneous. "Couldn't you get him to come over before he goes to New York?"

"I tried, but he was too busy."

"It's a shame we haven't gotten to know him before this. He insisted on paying for my coffee and cake at *Bottles* this afternoon."

All through the evening we half expected there'd be a phone call from Jake saying he and Edith would be coming along after all. But at eleven, when he still hadn't phoned, we settled instead for the national news. And there was that dark-haired journalist from New York again, making an intense plea for her people. Her devotion bordered on the kind of passion that possesses a lover.

Christine turned and looked at me.

"Well?" I asked.

"Well, what do *you* think?"

"Of course, that's not *her*," I said doubtfully.

"I think . . . I think it might be."

"Anyone might be."

"That's not true, Michael. But *she* might be."

I looked again at the intense, olive-skinned face on the TV screen. Her voice was childlike. It led you to her as if into a darkened garden with a crystal fountain at its centre. And then she was gone — replaced by some American automobile company proclaiming, as one car after another plummeted unharmed from a helicopter to the earth, that its cars, unlike the foreign competition, were *tough*.

"I guess we'll never know," I said.

But over the next three days all my doubts vanished. And an extraordinary few days they were too.

The most hectic, I thought, was the next day — Yom Kippur. Why do I do this? I asked myself, as I'd asked myself each year for decades when entering the *shiel*.

There was the stale smell of tobacco smoke in the lobby. An older worshipper nodded curtly to me to indicate where the prayer books were. He seemed like the same impatient worshipper I'd met at the synagogue ever since I was a child. And again I was looking at that ancient script thousands of years old: songs, pleas, pledges (*If I should forget thee, O Jerusalem, let my right hand lose her cunning, my tongue cleave to the roof of my mouth* — devastating disabilities, especially for a writer and teacher). People came and went; the cantor's voice rose in a cry from the heart, then was silent. It seemed that hours had passed, and suddenly I was aware that the synagogue was packed. The chatter about me had died down, and the air had become thick with anticipation. The moment had arrived, but seconds before the ram's horn was lifted, a whisper — loud, alarmed, surprised — sprang from the back doors and spread like a resonating echo from row to row. It rang with the ram's horn through the air and left us with a sense of disbelief. And then voices cried out in protest.

"What are you saying?"

"Yes, only a half hour ago. He was only two blocks from these doors."

"You saw it yourself?"

"Kaplan saw."

"But who knows for sure? From the hospital, what do they say?"

"For him there was no hospital."

"You're sure?"

That night all hope vanished into that fatal new year. The news flashed from street to street, from family to family, an unwelcome spirit visiting each house in turn with news of the heart attack that had refused to be denied any longer.

I thought again of Alfie Silverman, the young man, years ago, awakening in Las Vegas when he should have been awakening to a new life with his bride. And, in despair, sensing that all was lost, he'd fled to what was then Palestine to seek . . . only God knows what. And now Jake had also found the situation impossible — impossible to go on meeting his wife's eyes when she knew of his devotion elsewhere. What could he say to anyone else? To himself? Human hearts had not been made to suffer that kind of strain.

Two days later, the Jewish cemetery opposite Kildonan Park was so filled to overflowing you would have thought the Messiah himself had come. Everyone wanted a resolution, some understanding of this mystery. It was true, Jake had raced from responsibilities in Winnipeg to passionate infatuation in New York, but at the last he had listened to familiar voices. His mother, brother, chidren, wife, friends — all had had their piece to say, and at last he was drawn back from New York to his respectable house in Winnipeg. So why the sense of betrayal? And why were all those upset and outraged voices, innocent voices, labouring with an overwhelming sense of guilt?

About me, as I walked to the graveside, I could see in all directions neighbours and friends intermingling and moving among tombstones that no longer held just the names of strangers. No longer was the cemetery an essentially alien place. Over the decades, first one familiar name, then another, later a group in a rush appeared — as if each was determined not to be last and had all elbowed their way forward together, then in twos and threes again. Someday I expected, I would find more acquaintances there in the earth beneath than in the streets about me. Death itself would have become the old familiar neighbourhood, all part of the old gang, presences that would not go away but instead would beckon others to join their timeless community.

The coffin was brought forward, and I could hear Edith's voice break out — not only in grief, but now in anger also, a rage that seemed a scandal to all who were there — relatives and friends alike. Finally, though, she too grew silent.

From that silence rose the voice of the cantor, and with it returned the pain in my side — piercing, violent — that was determined to make its agonizing presence felt no matter what. As the voice rose and fell in its familiar chant, I became aware that there was one mourner apart from the others at the graveside. Nor did anyone turn to acknowledge her, or try to console her, though from the way she keened when the coffin was lowered into the grave, I could not doubt the intensity of her grief. And yet there was a beauty in her voice, too, and a clarity and strength of emotion that soared and rivalled the voice of the cantor. His eyes, though open wide with astonishment, seemed not to see her, even as his voice intertwined passionately with that of the dark-haired stranger.

The Getaway Car

Coming out to the West Coast was a first for me — in fact, a first for all of us. I was flying into Vancouver from Toronto, my Irish brother-in-law Fergus was driving in from Calgary with my sister Kate, and my parents from Winnipeg had driven to Victoria earlier in the summer for a year's sabbatical. From my limited perspective, it might appear the whole country was moving westward — lured by the siren song of the Pacific. Or were we all lemmings rushing off to our doom in the roar and swell of the sea? I'd bought the ticket for Vancouver rather than Victoria because the fare was so much cheaper. Besides, I had friends in Vancouver I'd met at Osgoode Hall, and I wanted to see them as well for a couple of days. At the end of the summer I would be starting my Bar Admissions course, but for the next two weeks I would be part of a family reunion on the West Coast. Also, while in Victoria I wanted to see Tom and Myra Gardiner. I had never met them, but what I'd heard about them from my parents was a constant source of amazement to all of us.

Two days after arriving in Vancouver, I said goodbye to my friends and cycled south down Highway 99 on my way to Tsawwassen, where I'd be catching the ferry to Victoria. The bicycle was a graduation gift I'd received from my parents. For $20 more I'd been able to bring it along on my ticket. But I could see I'd miscalculated how busy Highway 99 was, especially here at the outskirts of the city. Traffic, fed by the suburbs, roared by at an ever-increasing pace as I drew further and further away from Vancouver. In the congestion of downtown Toronto I'd more or less been able to keep up with the flow of traffic, but here cars rocketed by.

And what was that sign ahead? The Fraser River? The George Massey Tunnel? I'd never cycled through a tunnel before, but there's a first time for everything. The highway began to slope downward and soon I was doing over forty. Trucks cut in from feeder roads, buses honked, the tempo picked up, and there ahead I saw the dark opening of the tunnel into which we were all plummeting. Cars tore by me in the eerie fluorescent light, and the startled faces of drivers everywhere were staring at me in disbelief. Still the tunnel descended as the roar of traffic resonated shrilly. Behind me an immense trailer truck was trying to slow down, but without much success. The road had a film of water covering it like an emulsion. *Have to keep my balance somehow. But I can't slow down — or I'm dead. Must be tearing along at close to fifty.* And still we raced downward. Ahead I could see the grade of the road levelling out, and now it was beginning to take more effort to keep those pedals turning so quickly. That frantic thudding was my heart, and so much sweat was in my eyes I could barely make out the glint of metal on the road ahead. There was just time to comprehend the danger: *If my wheels slip through the slots in the grating, I'll be flung head over heels onto the pavement — and that trailer truck is still right behind me!* One moment of sheer terror, and the next moment I flashed by. Now I was working to keep the bike climbing up toward that widening halo of daylight. I did appreciate the fact that the trucker didn't honk at me all the way through the tunnel. He seemed as appalled by my witless bravado as I was myself.

Once out of the tunnel, the roar, louder than any ocean, gave way to the wet breath of the wind on my face, and to the celebration of sparrows, as I cycled up onto a sunny knoll that bordered the road. It was then I noticed the sign on the other side of the highway: NO BICYCLES ALLOWED! USE TRUCK SHUTTLE. There had to be another such sign where I'd entered the tunnel, though I hadn't seen it. I dropped to the ground in exhaustion and relief. This was one lemming that almost hadn't even made it to the sea.

Other bicyclists waiting for the ferry at Tsawwassen were astonished when they heard what I'd done. Had I cycled across the Rockies, too, they asked, ready now to believe anything? It was a curious journey, I reflected: by plane, by bicycle, and now by boat. Hours later, when I arrived at my parents' rented home in Victoria, I discovered that Fergus and Kate had driven in from Calgary the night before. I'd arrived just in time for lunch.

Everyone was sitting around the picnic table on the deck at the back of the house. And as I again related my adventure through the Massey Tunnel, the wonder in Mom's eyes was quickly replaced with alarm. All the while, she kept gazing first at me and then at my bike. At last she burst out, "That's incredible! You certainly didn't get that harebrained streak from my side of the family. It's all from your father's side . . . from the Buchalters. They're more than just eccentric; they're outrageous. Promise me you'll never do anything like that again."

"But, Mom, how will I get back?"

"By some other route, idiot! You speak to him, Michael."

Dad gritted his teeth in silence for a few moments, but under Mom's unrelenting gaze was at last compelled into speech. "Well, Christine, I must confess, when you first told me Joel was getting into a profession as cutthroat as law, I thought how will he ever survive? And as a criminal lawyer yet. But now I see he has no lack of the Buchalter *chutzpah* — along with their eccentricity." Then turning to me, he added, "You'll do fine, Joel. You know how to keep your eyes focused on what's ahead and you don't let yourself get pushed around by anyone bigger than yourself."

Despite herself, Mom started to smile. "That's not quite what I meant, Michael. Still, I want to thank you, anyway — yes, thank you! — for giving our son all that suicidal advice. Because I'm sure he has enough of me in him to survive anyway." Try as she had, though, to sound deadly serious, she could not help herself, and her every word was undercut with laughter.

Also at the picnic table, along with my sister Kate and her husband Fergus, were Tom and Myra Gardiner. I had been looking forward to meeting them ever since I knew I was coming out to the West Coast. Tom was explaining to Fergus about the fleet of cars he had stranded in the backyard and side driveway of his house. But Fergus's whole attention was focused on the way Tom, after finishing his meal, first lifted the plate to his mouth and, after licking it clean, proceeded to shine it up with his white beard.

"'Waste not, want not' is my motto," he declared by way of explanation. It soon became apparent that Tom's whole life was mapped out and charted by such family mottoes: "A stitch in time saves nine." "Seeing is believing." "Where there's a will, there's a way." "Better safe than sorry." I suspected the last motto had been added five years before, when Tom, as I'd learned from my parents, had loaned $30,000 to a friend who was opening an antique shop on Fort Street. The friend went bankrupt six months later. "But it wasn't his fault and we're still pals," Tom had explained, as if that excused everything.

"Mom tells me you were in the RCAF in the last war," Fergus said.

"For the whole six years," Tom replied.

"And your father invested all your money in stocks and bonds?"

"Yes," said Tom, taking off his old-style, wire-frame glasses to shine them clear — a seemingly impossible task. "He was kind of mean with money, my father was. 'A penny saved is a penny earned.' But he was right. The interest and rise in stock prices, plus the Veterans' Allowance, did let me study art at the University of Alberta."

"That's where I met him," said Myra. "I was the model for the class."

"The model?" asked Fergus.

"A nude model," Tom announced. "That's when I decided to marry her — during the first class. Sure didn't take me long to make that decision."

"That's the only decision in your life you've never procrastinated over," Myra laughed.

"Had my mind made up in not more than five seconds after she walked into the studio. I didn't even have time to rub my eyes. Zip, zap — and stop the world everyone! I'd never seen anyone step out of her clothes so fast before."

"And you've lived since then on your painting?" asked Fergus. "Are they all nudes?"

"No, some are landscapes, and the ones I didn't leave behind in Europe are at home here."

"But how do you live, then?"

"I've already told you," said Tom.

And when Fergus still looked puzzled, Myra added, "Since his days in the RCAF, Tom's never done an honest day's work. Our income is all from those stocks and bonds his father bought for him."

"Now that's not true, Myra. I did work in Kenya for seven years. You remember — that's when we became Quakers."

"Now, Tom, you know you spent most of those seven years meditating at the Meeting House, just waiting for inspiration — while I was out teaching school in the village."

To forestall the conversation continuing in that same vein, Tom turned to Fergus: "Christine tells me you're a mechanic."

"Since I was twenty. Back in Tipperary."

"Did you ever do anything else?" asked Tom.

"He was also a bartender," my sister Kate spoke up proudly.

"And why did you give it up?"

"Too hectic a life. It was a rough area of town, you know, and many's the time I was ducking punches while I was pulling pints."

"You wouldn't happen to have brought any of your mechanics' tools with you?"

"Always do. Never know when whatever old wreck I'm driving at the moment will fall apart."

"You wouldn't be interested in a little work out here? I know it's your vacation, but you don't want to get bored. You know what they say, 'The devil finds work for idle hands.'"

"True enough. I had to leave school at fifteen because the teacher claimed I'd set fire to the building."

"Well, about these cars of mine . . ."

"Oh, Tom," Myra interrupted. "You can't ask him to fix all those cars. Some of them haven't moved in fifteen years. And Fergus will find lots to do out here on vacation."

But Fergus's curiosity was aroused. "What kind of cars are they?"

"Every kind in the world," Myra laughed.

"There are two Morris Minors, a Dodge van, a Volkswagen, and a Volvo. I've also got a Datsun, but it's still running, though you might want to take a look at the clutch."

"What's wrong with the clutch?"

"Nothing much really, though hills are difficult. Can't quite make it to the top and then it starts rolling backward. Needs some adjustment, I guess."

"You need a new clutch, I expect, but that's not a problem."

"It's not?"

"No. I used to work for a Datsun dealer and all the mechanics'd have races to see who could replace a clutch the fastest. It got so I could have a new one in the car in forty-five minutes flat. But tell me about those two Morris Minors. What shape are they in?"

Suddenly I could see what was on Fergus's mind. Kate had always wanted a car of her own, and if Fergus got that fleet of old wrecks on the move once more, one of them would surely be hers.

"I would just be content," said Myra, "if you could get that Volvo going again. Now that was a comfortable car."

"It's still a comfortable car," insisted Tom. "Best place to read the *Globe and Mail*, right after breakfast, is in the back seat of that car. Keep checking up on our investments in the Business Section. And as long as I'm careful getting in and out, there's not much chance of the axles slipping off the blocks of wood they're balanced on."

I'd heard all about those infamous cars from my father, and from the glint in Tom's eyes behind those shiny spectacles I could guess at the kind of fantasy that was ablaze back there: a vision of all those rusting ruins starting into life, black smoke billowing again from exhausts, the neighbors gazing in wonder and astonishment as one car after another ripped itself free of weeds and enfolding branches and tore down the street, horns honking, lights flashing on and off as current coursed once again in electrical circuits unused for years. He would sell them to those doubting Thomases who had been saying they should all be towed off to the junkyard. And with the money bulging in his wallet, he could relax in a deck chair as Myra continued to reclaim the backyard from the junkheap it was always threatening to become. In her hands it would soon become Eden again, and then Tom would outline all his schemes to her as he sat sunning himself amidst all their blossoming fruit trees. Never again would a car be allowed back there. Not if Myra could help it.

I looked at Fergus — all six-foot-four of him — with his red hair and blue eyes. What made Myra sink back in her chair in despair had galvanized him, and I could see his large hands flexing in anticipation. He could hardly wait to get hold of a wrench and start to work on those cars.

"So let's hear about those two Morris Minors," he asked again.

"One of them is in a bad way — all rusted through. But the other wouldn't take much work to get going. The engine almost catches, but won't. Whatever's wrong is not much." Tom stared back into Fergus's eyes and a look of understanding passed between them.

"Well, Myra, we must be off," and Tom got to his feet. He was a relatively short figure — five-foot-six — and still moved with the ease of a slim person, though in fact he had a small pot belly.

By contrast, Myra was slim, had light blonde hair and still carried herself with a model's poise. "Now, Fergus, you're here on a vacation, so don't you let Tom browbeat you into getting all those cars going. They've been sitting in our backyard and driveway for at least fifteen years now and I expect they'll be there for another ten, unless you can convince Tom that they're beyond repair — all except for that Volvo, I mean."

But Fergus had bitten, I could see. And Tom knew it.

"Sure, let's have a look at that Volvo — and, while we're at it, we might as well check out the Morris Minor, too."

"And if they can't be fixed, I'd just like to see the last of them," sighed Myra.

"I'll come over tomorrow morning, first thing."

"But Fergus, we're going to the Pacific Rim tomorrow. Don't you remember? We were going to camp there till the weekend."

A look of impatience crossed Fergus's face, but then vanished. "The day after we're back, then, I'll be over bright and early."

After Tom and Myra had left, Fergus asked, "Don't you want that car, then, Kate?"

"My Dad's been telling me about Tom," Kate replied.

"Well, what does that mean?"

"You'll see."

I must confess that I didn't see what Kate was getting at either. But for the next few days I was content to bicycle all over Victoria. It was easy to see why the "Garden City" had such a magnetic hold on the rest of the country. One by one, certain images began to insinuate themselves into my mind, and absolutely refused to be dislodged — like the keel boat anchored off the southern shore at sunset. From my vantage point on the overlooking cliffs on Dallas Road, it had a look of quiet satisfaction about it. You felt there were people on-board sitting down to drink white wine and eat Pacific salmon caught only hours before.

Or, if not, there should have been. And then there was the view from Mount Douglas — another place I'd cycled to — that took in snow-capped mountains, sea, sailing boats, orchards and city streets. There was also the gentle and gracious manner of the people, whose gestures were those of a middle class that had once been the flower children of the Sixties. A most curious middle class. They had retreated to an island where they thought big business and industry could not readily follow.

But when I cycled inland on logging roads I discovered scenes of devastation that left me dazed: acres of tree stumps, abandoned logging chains and rusting machinery, the land churned into the kind of turmoil you usually witness on a stormy sea. And yet from the main highway, all that was visible was lush foliage, the occasional giant Douglas fir or red cedar, the look of a paradisal rain forest. The scene left me puzzling as I cycled back gloomily to Victoria. Was this what the siren call of the Pacific really had to offer?

By the time Kate and Fergus returned late Friday night, I'd had enough of cycling. I was quite prepared to surrender myself to Fergus's skill and the automotive age. But first I was to learn of their trip to Long Beach: of walks along the Pacific, mist rolling in along the shoreline, the icy waters that Fergus had plunged into again and again till he turned blue. All the way back to Victoria he'd spoken to Kate of selling off everything in Calgary and moving to the coast. But now, as we compared notes, that incadescence began to fade.

After a quick phone call the next morning that I'm sure roused Tom from his bed, we were off. When there was no answer to our knocking, we went around the house to discover Tom and Myra having breakfast in their backyard, a setting that was neither a garden nor a junkyard, but somehow a cross between. Myra was busy pouring tea, spreading home-made plum jam on toast, while Tom — bare chested, eyes closed — lay back on a chaise lounge in the sun like an Eastern potentate.

"Tom, wake up, we have company."

Tom's eyes remained closed.

"Tom, it's Fergus and Joel. They've come to fix our cars."

"Don't mind me," he murmured. "I want to catch the early morning sun. Here, you want to try some of this vitamin E lotion?" At last his eyes were open.

"What's that for?"

"I rub it on my chest, especially here. Helps me get a tan under my tits."

"Now, Tom, you mustn't tease them so. They don't know you that well yet. Fergus, Joel — would you like some breakfast?"

I could see that Fergus was ready to tear into those cars, but the scene was so beckoning — the garden chairs, the fragrance of the Earl Grey tea, the rich purple jam — that he let himself be diverted. Everything about this city had that effect. Whatever anyone's original intentions, just a few days within sight of the sea and mountains would begin to erode all human resolve. For Myra it was a triumph to keep Fergus relaxed there in the sun like a sleepy cat for half an hour, but then he rose to his feet.

"Now, let's see about those cars."

"I'll be along in a minute," Tom announced, reaching half-heartedly for his T-shirt.

Fergus strode out to the driveway to look first at the two Morris Minors.

"What are these boxes in the back seat?"

I climbed in and opened the cardboard flaps. "Books and magazines. A lot of *National Geographics*."

But Fergus wasn't listening. He already had the hood up. "Sweet Mother of God! Who's been messing with the engine?" And, as he came out from under the hood, "Who took the wheels off?"

"Didn't want the tires going flat," explained Tom as he joined us.

But now Fergus's eyes were focused elsewhere: at the crankshafts and pistons in the back of the Dodge van, at the valves and spark plugs and engine heads and camshafts and fuel pumps and fan belts all lying mixed together in cardboard boxes, at the nuts and bolts and transmission gears and clutch springs all lying in a tangle with gas filters and horns and disconnected radiators. All of it lay rusting in the morning sunlight. It was like an elephant burial ground.

"But why . . . ?" Fergus began when he was able to catch his breath.

"Some of the parts were broken and I had to raid other cars to try to substitute where I could."

Fergus's shoulders sagged. "A person could go *mad* . . . " he whispered.

"Well, how's it going, Fergus?" asked Myra as she came by with the breakfast tray in her hands.

Fergus's sagging shoulders managed a shrug. But the gesture was enough to confirm what she'd suspected for years.

"Perhaps you could get the Volvo going. Tom's left that one pretty well alone."

Fergus turned to the Volvo.

"The tires are in the garage," offered Tom, his voice ever hopeful.

Fifteen minutes later the wheels were on the car and we were pushing it onto the road.

"Joel, you steer the Volvo and I'll push it with my Datsun. It may take a block or two to get it going."

That was the understatement of the year. He pushed that car up Beach Drive to Cadboro Bay, back down Douglas to Beacon Hill Park, up and down every hill for miles around, it seemed, till finally we came charging up a road from which there was no exit, except over the cliff and into the sea. At the last moment I slammed on the brakes.

"Now what did you do that for?" called Fergus, tearing out of his Datsun, his eyes flashing with rage and frustration.

"Yes, let's do it," I said, reading his mind.

"Why not?"

"This car will never go. Not in this lifetime."

"And if we drive it back, somebody may be tempted to work on it again."

We both stood there, with the ocean roaring below and coaxing us on. The waves crashed and spray rose to cover us and the cars with a salt mist.

"Hold on. Maybe it's the compression," said Fergus. "I'll get my tester from the tool box. You hook up the jumper cables once I've pulled up alongside you."

A few minutes later the engine was turning over and Fergus was looking at his gauge. "Three of these cylinders are hopeless," he groaned.

"So what do we do?"

"Well, it's Tom's car . . . not for us to decide."

But as he spoke, the car started to roll forward, the horn began blaring and the headlights blazed into life. At once Fergus grabbed at the rear bumper and a moment later I was hanging on as well.

"Fucking son of a gun! Now it comes to life — all on its own!"

And it was true. It was as if, covered with spray and hearing the ocean, the car had decided never again to join the rusting ranks of its compatriots in Tom's side driveway, and now was clawing its way to the cliff's edge. All Tom's tinkering with the wiring and all that bouncing up and down the winding roads of Victoria must have, at the last, short-circuited the car into life. We let it drag us almost twelve feet before we let go. Slowly the front of the car tilted with the slope of the road, then picked up speed, and, after all these years, went racing — *racing* — down the cliff's side, where it struck a rocky outcropping and bounced forward into the air — and dropped over thirty feet into the water below. And now it was rocking with the swell of the waves, began to move away from the shore, and then vanished out of sight.

At that moment, as we stood there silent and aghast, there flashed through my mind the memory of my dash through the Massey Tunnel, the waters surging above me as my bicycle raced madly on — like the Volvo — and took on a life of its own. Together, we had raced for our lives through that fluorescent-lit tumult, while about us the West Coast had gaped in astonishment at our narrow escape from rust and ruin.

"The parking brake must have released," I said at last.

"Everything released. Even we released, at the end."

"But you must admit it was a rare moment."

"A great moment! But what will we tell Tom?"

"Tell Tom?"

"Yes."

"That while we were pushing the car, it coughed — once, twice — gasped, came to life and before either of us could get back in, it accelerated and made its escape."

"Do you think he'll understand?"

"I'm sure he will. After all, he's a free spirit too!"

Still we worried as we slowly made our way back in the Datsun to Tom's house. But I don't think either of us could have thought of a plausible story if we'd taken all summer to get back. When we turned the corner onto Lillian Street, there was Myra raking up the front yard. At her feet, Duke, their huge black cat, was leaping again and again into the enormous pile of leaves as if pouncing upon some succulent bird for his dinner. At the sight of the Datsun approaching, Myra looked up in anticipation, eyes smiling. Then she caught sight of me scrunched down in the passenger seat.

"But where's the Volvo?"

"It's a long story, Myra."

"You wouldn't want to know," added Fergus.

"Not in the junkyard! That was a comfortable car, I'll have you know. The best of the lot, and for you to take it off, without even asking, off to the junkyard . . . "

"It's not at the junkyard, Myra."

"But where then . . . ?"

"First tell us where Tom is," insisted Fergus.

"Where he always is — asleep in the backyard beside the compost heap."

"Well, the car too is now resting."

"Resting? Where?"

"Do you and Tom ever walk along the cliffs near here?" I asked.

"At least once a week."

"Well, the next time you're by that way, you might want to look out to sea."

"Out to sea? The Volvo?"

"Yes, *Rocked in the cradle of the deep*," sang Fergus in a mock bass voice.

"We couldn't help it, Myra, honest. We weren't expecting it to start and when it did . . . it . . . it just got away on us," I ended lamely.

In Myra's eyes we must have appeared like two inept schoolboys. But she didn't get mad at us. Instead, she laughed and invited us again into the backyard, where we spent the rest of the afternoon drinking beer and arguing with Tom about whether or not all the remaining wrecks should be towed off to the junkyard, or, if he preferred, we could drive them into the sea as well.

"But that other Morris Minor is worth a try," insisted Tom.

"No, it isn't," countered Fergus just as firmly. "It might be worth a trip up to the cliffs, but not much further."

"Damn it, that Volvo still had life in it."

"Once upon a time, maybe. And certainly at the last."

"Now, Tom, you have to agree to let those cars go," said Myra. "They've been cluttering up the backyard long enough. I want my garden back."

"But that Dodge van," persisted Tom. "Surely something could be done with that."

"Oh, yes," countered Fergus, "something could be done and, right after I finish this beer, Joel and I will be only too happy to do it."

In the end, Tom was content to be told again and again of how the Volvo looked at the last.

"You say it kind of reared up as it went over the cliff?"

"As full of life as ever," I assured him.

"The headlights were on?"

"And the horn was blaring too," Fergus added.

"And the wheels spinning?"

"And the engine racing," I reminded him.

"A grand sight!"

"Its finest moment," Fergus concluded.

"What a shame I wasn't there. Would almost have been worth it to be at the wheel when it tore up the cliff and made its last wild leap. That car sure used to have a lot of zip to it."

"If you're game, we could come over tomorrow morning and have a go with that Dodge van."

"You're kidding."

"Tomorrow morning at eight," said Fergus, draining his glass.

"At least let me *phone* the wrecking yard," said Myra, determined to press her advantage now that she had Fergus's backing. Duke had settled on her lap, and she'd begun to stroke him thoughtfully. "You know, Tom, we'll have to do something with all those wrecks when we sell the house next year and move to Barcelona."

"You're moving to Barcelona?" asked Fergus.

"Next spring." Tom was lying back in the chaise lounge and looking so rooted in the scene that it was impossible to imagine such a transition.

"Friends of ours are there now working on the house. We've been sending them money for years."

Fergus and I looked at one another in alarm.

"How much have you sent them?" asked Fergus.

"How much would you say, Myra? About $18,000?"

"That sounds right."

"And you've never seen this house in Barcelona?" Fergus was astonished.

"We have letters from Manuel and Maria describing all that they've done. The house will be owned jointly by both families."

"You just have their word?" The budding lawyer in me was suspicious.

"And the photographs," added Myra.

"Photographs?" Better than nothing, I thought.

"Yes," said Myra. "Now don't be so sceptical. Here, I'll show you," and a few moments later she returned from the house with the snaps.

It did help to restore my faith in human nature to see that house, in picture after picture, gradually taking shape on a hillside overlooking the Mediterranean. The architecture was Moorish, with a courtyard and garden, and with rooms and walkways in a square about the flowing fountain at the centre of the house. In the distance, we could see the magical outlines of Barcelona. Still, I puzzled.

Next summer, if all went well, Tom might again be resting on a chaise lounge, but by then he would be in Spain, alongside the Mediterranean, the sound of water murmuring nearby, the golden sun turning the scene back into a Platonic garden. And this time Myra would have *her* way: no collecting of old wrecks which just needed a bit of tinkering to get going, no storing of ancient *National Geographic* magazines in cardboard boxes, and — above all — no compost heap, at least not in the centre of the garden.

The memory of those photos stayed with me for the rest of my stay in Victoria. *Nothing* could be that perfect, I was sure. Not even Myra would be able to stop Tom from rubbing Vitamin E lotion into his tits as he lolled about in the sun with the salt air on his face. Or, at the end of a meal, suddenly lifting the plate to his lips and licking it clean before wiping it into a sparkle with his beard. But perhaps I was doing him an injustice. Here I had been thinking of him rooted in his garden, lulled into golden dreams by the murmurings of the ocean, asleep on his chaise lounge beside the compost heap. And yet there was still an adventurous streak in him that could easily be reawakened, one that harboured plans that outshone any of ours. Barcelona, the Mediterranean, sunlight flashing on Moorish architecture and flowing fountains — all secretly whispered that perhaps he lived by a motto that he hadn't yet voiced aloud to any of us. In any case, he seemed determined that every last morsel of life would be licked clean, no matter how ridiculous it might appear to others. And when I thought of the ever-gracious Myra, I saw her presiding at a small white table in a garden that would always be her world, pouring tea into ivory cups, layering plum jam on golden biscuits freshly baked. Could there be a time when we would all be able to jettison the accumulated junk of a lifetime and at last seek out some paradisal garden?

The day I left I caught a lift with Kate and Fergus back to Vancouver. As we tore through the George Massey tunnel, I was again aware of the reverberating roar of traffic, the treacherous film of moisture on the road, the sharp sudden glint of a metal grating in the headlights, but this time my bicycle was safely tied to the roof of Fergus's car. Then we were at the airport and I was saying goodbye to sweet Kate and her wild Irish husband — goodbye to the West Coast where my parents would stay until the following year — and goodbye to Tom and Myra in their garden, with a compost heap not quite large enough to decompose Tom's fleet of rusting cars nearby. Ahead of me waited court appearances, legal arguments, and endless interviews with distraught clients that might well leave me feeling, at the end of several decades, at my wit's end. As I went through the security gate, pushed and jostled by the crush of people, and got on the plane, I was aware that most of my family was now scattered between two oceans. A crucial centre to my life I had always counted on was now gone. And when the plane leapt into the sky, that feeling grew stronger as one by one the images of the last two weeks began to fade. Except for one. And that one has grown more intense, more sharply outlined, as time has gone by. The Volvo — lights ablaze, horn blaring — leaps from the cliff's edge into space, into a new life, while below the sea crashes and roars its dangerous cry of welcome to me — and to us all.

How the Free Trade Act Almost Ruined
My Cousin's Bar Mitzvah

When my cousin Tessie phoned from Seattle, a week before Canada Day, to invite us to her son's bar mitzvah, I was not exactly overjoyed. Christine and I were staying in Victoria on sabbatical, and I was late with my project. It was 1988 and the Free Trade Debate was at its most frenzied; I was so strongly against the agreement that, frankly, for me to visit the US seemed hypocritical. But — more importantly — bar mitzvahs were treacherous occasions for me. Some families glory in them — even rush off to the Wailing Wall in Jerusalem for the celebration. Our family *stumbles* over them. As we do over most things.

Let me explain: my own bar mitzvah had pretty well proceeded without a hitch that memorable day in February, 1945, until, at the dinner that night, my mother insisted I repeat the same speech I had given that morning at the *shiel*. It was not a bad speech, the one Rabbi Hoffman had written for me: there were quotations from the prophet Elijah; parallels drawn between the career of Hitler (now rapidly drawing to a close) and the career of the Biblical Haman, who got himself hanged for a somewhat similar endeavour; and there were hopeful glimpses into the future. The only problem was that each and every guest at that dinner had already heard the speech earlier. And not just that morning, but at every bar mitzvah given during the last few months. Still, it was all good fun. If I could give a repeat of the well-known Rabbi's speech (which I was encouraged to believe I alone had composed), all the guests could once again recite the pieces of advice, heard time and time again at these events, each meant to provide incomparable delight, and edification, for the new bar mitzvah boy. With the warmth of the sweet, red wine flowing through us, we all pretended to an originality that simply did not exist.

Except for Uncle Yosel. Perhaps driven to a frenzy by the unremitting repetition that had not varied much over the last few months — or years — he leapt to his feet to denounce not only the occasion, but also me, the bar mitzvah boy himself. He was not thrown out, much less asked to leave. After the initial shock, his behaviour was simply put down to a spirit that had been eaten up with bitterness and spite. *Ameryka* had become for him the land, not of promise and fulfillment, but of endless failures, each more unremitting than the last. No doubt he felt he had a right to rage against anyone not similarly diminished. I suppose what must have hurt him most was that, while he strove for a prophetic fury, he was aware how, in the eyes of all who'd known him these past years, he was a bigger disappointment than ever. And so, our own Elijah had stepped forth and tried as best he could to turn the wine of celebration into vinegar.

Still, the occasion was etched into my memory because I had finally learned why some bar mitzvahs *should* be held at the Wailing Wall.

But Christine wouldn't hear of refusing Tessie's invitation. "For God's sake," I reminded her, "you're not even Jewish."

"Shh," she put her finger to her lips, "you knew that when you married me."

But we were still arguing on the way towards the border crossing at Blaine, Washington.

"You remember that last bar mitzvah we were at for my nephew Yitzchok in Winnipeg?"

"Of course."

"It was embarrassing," I insisted.

"What was embarrassing?"

As we waited in the lineup that led to the customs booth, the scene came vividly back to me. We were in the synagogue reception hall for the luncheon. Beside me, my mother was in a desperate, give-no-quarter argument with my Aunt Fanny, who sat across from her. My mother couldn't believe her ears.

"You say your new son-in-law Alex has a Ph.D. in aeronautical engineering?"

"Of course. My Tessie says that all PROFESSIONALS have Ph.D.'s now. Anything less is like . . . like . . . KINDERGARTEN!" The words were blurted out — trumpeted in a note of triumph.

At once my mother was on the defensive. "But, still, my Michael has a Master's Degree. From Toronto, yet!" she beamed triumphantly.

"Master's — schmasters!" My aunt, who'd never learned to read or write in her native Russian, let alone in English,

was clearly not one to let educational standards be lowered.

"Why do you laugh?" my mother prodded me angrily. "Say something!"

"What is there to say?"

My Aunt Fanny glowed, her turn again to triumph.

"Say!" my mother insisted. Suddenly I was a thirteen year old, grade-seven pupil whose excellence was once more being debated within the higher circles of the family hierarchy.

Then, spurred to fury by my continued silence, my mother struck. "I suppose if he — your new son-in-law Alex — if he can't get a job with just an M.A., he has to go back to school again — and *repeat!* But my Michael, he doesn't need to *repeat* his school work and get a Ph.D. With an M.A. — from Toronto! — it is more than enough for him to get a job. And not just any job, but to teach at the University."

My Aunt Fanny looked stunned. *"A REPEATER!"* she screamed with a voice that froze the rest of the table into silence. "You're saying my new son-in-law Alex — my Tessie's husband — is a REPEATER?" she demanded.

"What? Your Tessie didn't tell you?" my mother lunged for the kill. "For sure — he's a REPEATER! At school they are holding him over."

My Aunt Fanny — all red-faced — looked to me for help. Desperately I turned to my father. But he too was engaged in a battle of sorts. Across the table from him sat Mr. Waldman, a business rival.

"What did your wife say?" Mr. Waldman was demanding. "Your son teaches at the university?"

"Yes," proclaimed my father proudly, "and he has already two promotions."

"Then where," began Mr. Waldman with that North End inquisitorial tone I knew all too well, "where did you get your Ph.D.?" he asked, turning to me.

Again I explained.

"No, no," Mr. Waldman attacked at once. To my father, he announced triumphantly, "Without a Ph.D. your son cannot teach at a university. Maybe at an elementary school! But not at the university."

Clearly, if the North End had been on my tenure committee, I would have quickly been given the bum's rush.

"Tell him," my father demanded.

Again I felt as if I were expected to repeat my bar mitzvah speech. And I knew where *that* would lead.

"Alright, so it was embarrassing, Michael, but don't be silly. Tessie would be insulted if we didn't come to Danny's bar mitzvah."

"Where are you headed?" We had just arrrived at the US immigration booth.

"Bothell. Just above Seattle."

"And how long will you be here?"

"Just two days."

"Welcome to the USA! Enjoy your visit." And we were waved on.

We arrived Friday night, and early the next morning we were at the synagogue. And I must confess, it all went swimmingly — despite the fact that we had stayed up into the early hours of the morning arguing about the Free Trade Act.

"What have you got against Americans?" Tessie had demanded as we battled — at first politely, then savagely — through the early morning hours. "I think they're pretty nice. I even married one. In case you hadn't noticed."

"I don't have anything against Americans. But this is a disastrous deal for us. The whole industrial sector will pick up and move south of the border."

"So what's wrong with that? They'd probably become more efficient and produce better goods."

"It'll set the country back a hundred years."

"That's impossible! The country's already a hundred years behind where it should be. You Canadians are so timid. Always scared to take a chance. No wonder nothing really important ever happens up there."

"Oh, cut it out, Tessie. Next thing I know you'll be singing 'The Stars and Stripes Forever'."

"Michael!" Christine warned. "Alex will feel insulted. Don't forget, you told me yourself he's an ex-Marine. He fought for that flag."

Alarmed, I looked toward Alex, but with a wave of the hand he indicated there were no hard feelings.

You would have thought, at that point, Tessie and I would have let the argument rest, but like true North Enders, we were just getting wound up. By three in the morning, we must have sounded more and more like Mr. Waldman and Aunt Fanny. I'm sure that if we'd continued another ten minutes, Tessie would have blurted out something irretrievable like, "Well, if that's the way you feel about Americans — and don't forget my son Danny *is* an American now — just don't bother staying for his bar mitzvah." And, of course, I would have felt compelled to snarl out something equally unforgiveable, like, "Who would want to hang around for some crummy bar mitzvah, anyway? Christine and I are leaving right now!"

But later that morning, hardly able to keep our eyes open and certainly not daring to glance at one another, there we all stood at the *shiel*. Danny read the passages from the Torah without a hitch and afterward made his speech — in which again there were references to Elijah and Haman, but with President Assad as a reincarnation of Hitler. Then he collected all his presents at the luncheon which followed and disappeared with his friends for the rest of the day. God, I thought, my American cousins sure do know how to cope easily with these things.

That afternoon, as we sat in Tessie's living room, I continued to be astonished by her grace and ease. To be totally frank about the matter, grace and ease were about the last two words in the English language that I would have thought could be associated with either my cousin Tessie or myself. But now I saw that in our encounter the previous evening, we had each reverted to the behaviour of an earlier era. And, in the heat of battle, nothing that either of us said had seemed out of character.

As a matter of fact, through most of our years of growing up together in Winnipeg, I'd known Tessie as someone bogged down by a bungling manner that left her reeling from one social disaster to another. In fact, she managed to bungle just about every opportunity that came her way.

Then, in a desperate counterattack — as if to prove she was not totally devoid of taste and grace — she'd taken Fine Arts at university. And, to everyone's astonishment, in her final year, she'd won the Gold Medal. Then — another miracle — that summer she'd become engaged to Irwin Steinkopf, who — praise God! — was a graduate pharmacist. And, what's more, he even ran his own drugstore! Her mother's prayers, it seems, had been answered. No more Wailing Wall for her! Except that, ten years later, Tessie again astonished the whole North End by picking up and leaving Irwin and going to Los Angeles with her eight-year-old son, Danny. That innate blundering quality, that unerring sense of always making the wrong decision, had not, it seemed, been jettisoned.

But in Los Angeles, despite the prophecies of doom being trumpeted in Winnipeg, she'd not only remarried — "Impossible!" people scoffed — but she'd gotten a job at a posh private school with only her Bachelor of Fine Arts degree. "We don't believe it!" the usual North End crowd roared. And when her mother, out of desperation, claimed that Tessie had gotten her Ph.D. through a correspondence course taken in the evenings, she was hooted down with laughter. One of Tessie's aunts — her mother's arch-enemy — was the worst. "Everyone knows there are no Ph.D's in Fine Arts," she shrilled. "Such a schmaltzy subject. It's not IMPORTANT enough!"

But here, looking at Tessie now . . . well, *stunning* was the only word. Her eyes were dark and vibrant, her face like sculptured marble, and the clothes she wore flowed in long, symmetrical lines. There was not a hint of that clumsiness and awkwardness that could trip her up in Winnipeg when she seemed only a step away from some triumph.

"So you like being an American?" I asked as we sat in Tessie's living room after Danny had dashed off with his friends.

"I love it!"

Across from her in his easy chair, Alex grinned. "Things have worked out for us since we moved here to Seattle." He was a hefty guy — about 220, I'd guess — and built like an all-star football player.

"You like it better than Los Angeles?"

"Boeing pays more than Lougheed and the work is more interesting."

"So neither of you regret the move?"

"God, no," Tessie added. "I've gotten a part-time job as an art instructor with the university here, and my shows keep selling out. I've become a success, Michael, a success!" She sounded more surprised than I was.

(I could imagine the same North Enders — Mr. Waldman, in particular — scoffing. "You say she has a university job with just a Bachelor of Fine Arts? Impossible! Don't tell such stories!")

"Honestly, you will hear of me," my cousin Tessie promised.

Again, I looked at Tessie. Was this the same person I'd always known? I recall her puzzling years ago at a cousin's bar mitzvah in Winnipeg: "It's true. We Buchalters must be the most awkward, the most bumbling of all the immigrants in the North End. And the North End is not exactly the seat of graciousness, you know." It was said, not as a criticism, but as a confession, a description of her own condition. All her wit and charm were then caught up in a continuing battle with her blundering manner. Though if anyone could win that battle, I now saw that Tessie was the one to do it. And, yes, she had succeeded: she'd leapt into the American melting pot, and emerged *transformed*. As she leaned back in a green lounge suit in her sunken living room, with light flooding in gently from the skylights above, I marvelled at her.

"How do you like our house?" she asked proudly — really meaning: "How do you like my new life?"

"It's an amazing house," I said.

"Was it hard to find?" asked Christine.

"Not at all," answered Alex.

"But it must take some getting used to," I remarked. "Especially that stream running through the backyard. It's a park back there."

"A full acre," explained Alex.

Finally, I could hold back no longer, and speculated on what such a house would cost in Toronto. Or in Victoria, for that matter.

"Frankly," said Alex, "when the agent showed me the place, I didn't think we could afford it. And then, when he told me $125,000, I thought there must be some mistake."

"What did you say?"

"Well, I was so taken by surprise that I simply blurted out, 'What — for the *whole house?*'"

"And what did the agent say to that?"

"He kind of choked up and I'd swear he turned pale, but finally he nodded. Right then and there, I shook his hand — it was trembling. 'It's a deal,' I said, and that afternoon I arranged a small mortgage with the bank."

"From the minute I stepped across the border my life changed," said Tessie in a voice which conveyed some of her own continuing surprise. "But tell me," she went on, returning to the topic that had gotten us arguing almost the whole night and almost ruined my cousin's bar mitzvah. "Just why is there all this resistance to the Free Trade Bill? It's bound to be to the advantage of both countries.

Why won't you agree? We Yankees are not such a bad lot. We're pretty fair about these things."

I recalled the furor that had been raging in Canada during the last couple of months. "We just don't want to become Americans," I finally said.

"But you know, Michael, whenever I go back to Canada — to an art show in Vancouver or to see old friends in Winnipeg — I have the sense that everybody there is moving underwater. So slowly. So carefully. And inevitably very little actually gets done. Anything important gets argued about endlessly, and examined from every angle instead of being acted upon. Nothing's changed there. I feel as if it's a country that will freeze up with indecision every time a real opportunity comes along. You'll even bungle this Free Trade Act. And it *is* an opportunity."

"Have you been back lately?"

"Just last spring. To Winnipeg, to see some old friends," she added. "I also looked in on Irwin."

Irwin, I recalled, was her ex-husband, the pharmacist.

"How is Irwin these days?" I asked, determined to get onto some topic other than the Free Trade Act.

"You know he's gotten married again?"

"No, I didn't."

"He got married to a pretty little clerk in one of his drugstores. She must be half his age."

"When?"

"Only days after our divorce finally came through. I guess he was stunned when I left. And he wanted to prove something. He was the only one who would look at me when we got engaged. You remember the sort of thing I was always doing: spilling red wine on a friend's new chesterfield, blocking the sink with coffee grounds, dropping the guest towel in the bathroom down the toilet. And then always adding to the mess with this sharp tongue I have. For years after Irwin and I were married, I was so grateful to be out of that state of mind that I didn't realize I was suffocating. He was just never around. Weekends, holidays — always at that damn drugstore. But then, one bitter winter five years ago, while I was chopping ice off the windshield, I made a promise to myself, 'This is the last time I'll ever do this — the very last time.' And it was. I left Irwin and all that ice and snow in January and went to Los Angeles. That's where I met Alex."

"So things have worked out then? For both you and Irwin, I mean."

"Oh, Irwin still has problems."

"What problems?"

"The kind of problems that come from running a drugstore: people wanting drugs."

"Can't he just tell them no?"

"Well, it's kind of hard with someone waving a pistol in your face."

"Irwin told you this?"

"He still has the scars. Two robbers wearing balaclavas came in last winter and demanded drugs. When he made the mistake of saying no, they pistol-whipped him."

"I didn't think those things really happened, except on the late news."

"It was happening to both of us before I left, if you know what I mean. That's why I was so determined not to leave Danny behind with his dad."

"I can see that America agrees with both of you."

"Well, it wasn't always so easy, was it, Alex?"

At my puzzled glance, Alex said, "When I met Tessie I was out of a job. I think every aeronautical engineer in the country was out of work then."

"How come?" I remembered my Aunt Fanny's boast about Alex's degree in aeronautical engineering.

"Cutbacks in defence. The space shuttle disaster. Everyone was looking for work. And there was Tessie moving into my apartment block with her son. I'd never seen anything like it: that assurance, the kind of effortless way she got a green card. Not that easy these days, believe me." The person he described did not sound like the Tessie I knew. Certainly not the Tessie who gained instant notoriety in the North End when she totalled her father's car the first time she took a driver's test.

"And then she got a job as an art instructor at a private school. Just like that!" And here Alex snapped his fingers to show how effortless her achievement had been. "All the while my savings kept disappearing till I didn't know what I'd do."

"What *did* you do?" asked Christine.

"He used to come upstairs to my apartment on the weekends and I'd feed him."

"Finally, I was so desperate that I would have taken anything."

"And?"

"And a sort of job did come along, but I didn't know what to do."

Here Tessie interrupted: "But I said, 'What's to know? A job's a job. Take it.'"

"What kind of job?" I asked.

"There was no steady salary," Alex explained. "It was all commission work."

"As a salesman?"

"No . . . " Alex began, obviously sorry now that he'd let the conversation drift in this direction.

"So what kind of work did you do?" asked Christine finally with a bluntness that left him startled.

"Well, it has to do with the legal system."

"You delivered a summons to a person hard to locate?"

"No, actually it had to do with bail."

"With bail?"

"Yes, with people who would skip out on their bail. I'd have to bring them back."

"You mean you were a *bounty hunter?*" Christine laughed.

"I guess so."

"Wasn't that kind of dangerous?"

"Alex used to be a Marine," said Tessie.

"But still . . . "

"I always carry a gun. A person-stopper. A magnum."

Both Christine and I were stunned. Once you crossed that border, you sure knew you were in the States, alright. Who said the Wild West was dead?

"How long did this go on?"

"My legal work, you mean? I worked on commission for about a year. Then the job opened up with Lougheed."

"And we got married," added Tessie. "But while we were in California, the agency still kept phoning him up. To track down some real slippery types. Alex had gotten really good at it, but by then I was getting fed up and I said, 'Enough!' I was relieved when we finally came up here to Seattle."

"But why are we sitting around? Would you like to see the place where I work?"

"You mean the Boeing plant?" Good, I thought, better than spending the rest of the weekend arguing about the Free Trade Act.

"It's just a few miles down the road."

"Love to," said Christine.

And so we were off. As we all squeezed into the Chevette, Alex explained: "It's a rental. My Oldsmobile got totalled last week on Interstate 5. In fact, I'm lucky to be around this week for Danny's bar mitzvah."

"Don't be silly. You're indestructible," insisted Tessie. "You're a Marine. A warrior."

"A bounty hunter!" added Christine, teasing.

We were out of the park-like surroundings now and headed toward Interstate 5.

"Don't laugh," insisted Tessie. "I hunted up the Teitelbaum family tree. They were warriors during the golden age of the Austrian-Hungarian Empire. His great-grandfather is even mentioned in a book I found in the YMHA library: *A History of Europe — from a Jewish Perspective*, by Irving Kunstler."

"In a footnote," scoffed Alex.

"A Jewish warrior?" I asked. "A knight? Sir Alex Teitelbaum?"

"Tessie gets carried away with these things," Alex laughed. "You should see the painting she's done of me in my Marine uniform."

"It's a composite painting," Tessie explained. "He's packing a six-gun and wearing a Stetson. And standing in front of the Boeing plant like . . . like a cowboy in front of a saloon."

"Well, your warrior got really creamed last week on this highway," Alex remarked. "Right about here," and he pointed to a barely discernable maze of skid marks on the asphalt where a feeder road cut into the lane beside us. "It was a five car smash-up, with glass and antifreeze all over the place — and bodies. But that Oldsmobile did save me. So as soon as I got to the hospital, I phoned the dealer and ordered a new one."

"You ordered a car on the phone?" Christine asked.

"I just don't have the time to go shopping," Alex explained. "I've been working double shifts. In fact, I haven't even had a chance to sign the papers and pick it up yet. Meanwhile, I'm making do with this rental." He stepped on the gas and soon we were on the road skirting the Boeing plant.

"What's that?" Christine pointed to a flat-topped structure fairly low to the ground that stretched off into the distance.

"That's where I work."

As we sped closer, we saw that one of its massive doors was open, and within we could see the nose of a gleaming silver fuselage under construction. We drove closer still, and now we could see the roof towering above us.

"An optical illusion," explained Alex. "It's actually eleven stories high and the building covers five acres."

"And Tessie's painted you standing in front of it?"

"With a fighter plane just behind him," said Tessie. "Except that with all the gold light and shadows, he looks as if he might be a statue standing at the entrance to a royal tomb."

"Look, Tessie," asked Alex, "would you mind if I drove round to the side entrance?"

"Not overtime. Not again."

"I may have to go in tomorrow."

In silence we drove round that mammoth structure. It took about five minutes before we arrived at the office door, and once Alex stepped within, it was if he he'd never existed. We waited ten minutes. Then another twenty minutes passed. Finally I said, "Look, Tessie, maybe I should go in and see what's up."

"There's no point," she replied. In her voice I sensed something I'd never heard before. An acceptance of something massive and silent against which it was useless to struggle. Like an historical process that was inevitable. Eventually, when it was time, I suppose, Alex emerged.

Tessie's look was a question and he replied, "I have to go in tomorrow."

"But it's Sunday!"

"So what else is new?"

"But we were going to take Michael and Christine to see the 'Son of Heaven' exhibit in Seattle tomorrow. It's a once-in-a-lifetime opportunity. We can catch it anytime during the next month, so for us it doesn't matter that much, but they can't."

"Boeing isn't interested."

"Oh, there are times I wish we were back in Los Angeles."

"And that I was still a bounty hunter?"

"It would be better than this helpless feeling I get sometimes."

"You can still go into Seattle."

"Without you?"

"Why not take Danny with you?"

So it was settled. The next morning long before we were up, Alex had already vanished into that massive structure — one among thousands of civilian combatants — into the largest building in the world. It was as if he had been swallowed whole.

"Michael," Danny asked at breakfast, "do you think I could drive us into Seattle? I've never driven a Honda before."

"But you're only thirteen . . . " I began.

"Danny," began Tessie, "I told you not to ask."

"But Dad lets me drive the Oldsmobile all over the state."

"He does?"

"All the kids here zip around in the family car," explained Tessie. "And especially now that Danny's had his bar mitzvah . . . "

"At my bar mitzvah, all I got was a fountain pen," I protested. "That's all anyone ever got!"

"Here they take over all the available cars," Tessie sighed.

"Perhaps on the way back," I began. Immediately Christine looked at me in alarm, but the words were out and there was nothing to be done.

I needn't have worried. On the way into Seattle, Danny provided expert advice as to which cut-offs to take, and which streets to turn down. Unhesitatingly we surged forward into the crowded traffic and made our way to a tiny, well-hidden parking lot less than a half block away from the Civic Centre. "Dad lets me drive this route all the time," he boasted.

"Only during the last month," Tessie insisted.

Danny was a loose-jointed, big-framed kid, and already I could see that he would develop a build far more powerful than his father's. There was a gangling quality to his walk and he was always rushing off ahead of us and then returning — an engaging smile on his face — to announce which entrance to take, where the gift shop was, or where we could get tickets to the "Son of Heaven" exhibit. But once we were within those darkened halls, his boisterousness vanished and his energy was focused on everything about us.

Displays were lit up in the darkness to reveal models of ancient temples, all in gold, ferocious warriors guarding palace entrances, silver swords, glimmering armour, yellowing manuscripts, and, at last, the four terracotta warriors. They stood before us, magical, over six feet tall, each fashioned more than twenty-one hundred years ago after an actual person. And then they and the hundreds of skilled artisans who created them were killed and buried in the trench surrounding the emperors' tombs. And now at last these warriors had emerged, not just from the flames that a rival emperor had ordered to be set, but also from corruption itself — for the fire had served to harden the clay. These conquerors of time, still looking about them with their characteristic glances, were ready to challenge their new world. Light seemed to radiate from them while we turned into mere shadows. Another age — golden and majestic — had emerged from the earth and now traversed oceans and nations. Those warriors followed us from exhibit to exhibit: invisible presences. Finally it was time to leave — the moment I had been dreading since my rash promise that morning. Danny guided us through the maze of streets and lanes, and there was the parking lot hidden between several large warehouses. I had been steeling myself for the request I knew would be coming, but Danny said not a word. As we neared the car, I surprised myself — and Christine — by flipping him the keys, and we were off.

There was no racing to make a light or swerving to get around slower cars. Expertly Danny followed the signs to the freeway, turned onto the ramp, and now we were back on the Interstate. The tricky part was over. We powered along in the midst of the swarming traffic. And even though it was Sunday, not an inch of extra room was available. About us cars tore by impatiently. I was reminded of the frenzied freeways in Toronto and Detroit.

If even one spark plug should fail to fire, we'd be dead. And just as the thought entered my mind, I felt the car falter.

"What's the matter?" Christine asked, alarmed.

"I don't know."

Oh God, we're in for it now.

But Danny refused to get flustered. On went the blinker lights, and we were expertly nudging our way over three lanes of traffic to the shoulder. About us there was the screeching of brakes, the alarm of horns — traffic hesitated a moment, and then the surge continued, like water in a stream swerving around a stone — and we were safely coasting to a stop on the side of the road.

For the moment we were safe, but it was not a good situation. In the past I had seen cars stranded on highways and freeways and puzzled how anyone ever managed to get going again. The stream of traffic was unending. Thank God we were not in New York City. There, scavengers would have already been pulling over to strip the car clean. I recalled the story Alex had told of his brother's car breaking down and coasting to a halt. While looking under the hood he felt the car move, and, looking up, he saw that someone was already jacking up the back in order to remove the wheels. "Hey, what're you doing?" he shouted.

"It's okay — it's okay, Mac. You take the front end and I'll take the back."

Still, even outside of Seattle, it was not a good situation to be in. How will I ever find a phone? Where do I find a garage that's open on Sunday?

"How do you pop the hood open?" Danny wanted to know.

"It takes a trained mechanic to sort out what's in there, Dan."

"Just thought I'd take a look."

In a moment, he was doing something with the wiring and then he signalled for me to try the starter. The engine kicked over energetically enough, then died.

"Michael, do you think it's safe to let him try to fix it?"

"Don't worry," said Tessie. "He's always offering to tune up Alex's car. And sometimes Alex lets him."

I could see Danny looking intently again at the maze of wires under the hood; then he took a cable and pushed it in place. Again, he signalled.

The car started with a roar. In moments, the hood was down and Danny was settled triumphantly back in the car.

"What was it?"

"The central cable to the distributor had worked its way loose. Just needed to be pushed back in so it could make contact."

What ever happened to all of Tessie's clumsiness? Her ineptness? Not a sign of any of it now — certainly not in Danny.

Again, he had the signal lights on as we watched the unending line of traffic tearing up behind us. Soon Danny had us rolling along the shoulder at about sixty, and when one car hesitated for a moment, we swung in front of it onto the highway and at once were part of that relentless flow. A half hour later, we pulled off the Interstate and were soon into the park-like surroundings of Tessie's place.

As we got out of the car, sunlight from the trees around the house was filtering down about us. In that golden glow, we were all still for a moment — silent. We all knew it might be years before we saw one another again and we wanted to retain this moment. I looked at Danny, and the words of his bar mitzvah came back to me: "And now I am a man." The words — whether spoken by myself or by countless, equally scrawny cousins — had always seemed slightly ridiculous. But not this time. I could see even now the kind of man Danny would become. Then the spell was broken and we were collecting our luggage for the drive back to Victoria.

"Stay the night, why don't you?" asked Tessie. "Alex should be back in an hour or so. You're not angry, are you, about those critical things I said about Canada? That Free Trade Act will be a godsend, you just wait and see."

"Of course we're not angry, but we have to be starting back."

"Then I'll get on with my painting. There's a show in New York I want to be in next summer."

Something in her voice — as if it were already a reality — swept away all doubts. "We'll meet again next year in New York, then. All of us."

"And pity the car highjacker or mugger who comes at us with Alex around."

"Someone else having to get bail."

"Don't be mad at me, Michael."

"Oh, Tessie."

Abruptly, she flung out her arms and rolled her eyes at the heavens in the way I could recall her instinctively doing whenever she jarred people's composure with some impossible new blunder.

The car started at the first turn of the ignition key, and now we were coasting down the hill and onto the road that led to the Interstate.

Three hours later we were back in Canada at the border crossing in a long line-up waiting to get through Customs. Behind us the Olympic Range rose in its mantle of snow and clouds. Ahead, just across the border, roamed students from UBC distributing pamphlets warning against the effects of the Free Trade Act.

What a blunder for those students to be coming here, I thought. They won't get a sympathetic hearing from this crowd. Not from these people waiting around forever in cars loaded to the rafters with all the goodies they've just bought.

"Don't let Mulroney do it!" pleaded a young girl with blonde hair reaching down to her waist. "Don't let him sell out the country!"

Silently I took the pamphlet from her. Her eyes held mine for a moment before she turned to another car. What did they think of us, these students, as they saw us drifting back across the border? These Canadians who fled to the States at the first opportunity? And to what? To five-car pile-ups on the freeway? To a land where bail jumpers scampered for their freedom from ex-Marines out of work? I thought of Alex and those thousands of other workers vanishing into that vast tomb of a factory, the white building like a sepulchre. Would they all be dug up one day to be marvelled at by a future generation: silent artifacts still inhabiting a technological microcosm? Had that note I'd heard in Tessie's voice outside the Boeing factory been one of dread?

Then we were at Customs. "Have you bought anything during your stay? Anything of value?"

At our silence, the Customs officer asked again, "What have you brought back?"

"Just ourselves."

While he mulled that over, I looked into the rear-view mirror and saw a silent army of students waving placards. They were everywhere, moving along all four lanes of stalled traffic. Then as we were waved forward, I recalled Tessie's words once more: "Nothing's changed back there. When I went back last summer, people were moving around as if they were underwater. Everything gets done so slowly." For her, it was Canada that was buried underground, drowned in some subterranean cave, until someday it would have to make its way up into the air and sunlight again.

Then I stepped on the gas, leaving behind the student protest against the Free Trade Act, a protest which had only made me all the more aware of the country struggling to emerge out of subterranean shadows and take on a human shape once more.

A Memorial for Johnny

My tears stream down —
To whom can I confide my sorrow?

Still pursuing Johnny, I took the ferry to Victoria and tramped the streets of Chinatown. *Which buildings, which houses once served as rooming houses for the immigrant Chinese?*

As with many prairie dwellers, my trip to the West Coast was a search for Shangri-la, but my more serious purpose was to understand those wandering shades of the past — the palely smiling Chinese in shoddy workman's clothing that haunted me still. Earlier, on the campus at UBC, I had glimpsed them in the faded photographs, taken in the early part of the century, that lined the walls of Asian House. *Could one of these young men be Johnny?* I had first known him when he was nearly fifty: the gentle dispenser of clean, ironed laundry for our family's use. And even then, as a young boy growing up in Winnipeg's North End, I sensed, within that lined oval face and hard wiry body, the troubled kinship bestowed upon us by historical coincidence and the vagaries of chance.

"Rooms that were cubicles? Rented at $4.00 a month?" All my inquiries in Victoria were met by puzzled looks. The Chinese I spoke with were too young: in their thirties or forties. I needed someone in his eighties or early nineties, but when at last I found him, I was met with an uneasy stare and a garble of Chinese sprinkled with only a few words of English.

Johnny had said he would return, if not to China, then here to Victoria to die. But to ask for Johnny the Laundryman from Winnipeg — formerly from Kirin Province, the town of Yantsi — was a futile task. Still I wandered from shop to shop, down narrow alleyways, into a dusty Chinese bookstore; into a shop smelling of lavender and filled with trinkets and with what looked like apothecary jars of rare herbs and powders, such as are made from ground rhinos' horns and tigers' bones; then into an art gallery whose basement was filled with woven baskets, hats, trunks, exotic birds, horses with wings, and a fire-breathing dragon. At last, having listened to puzzled voices for days on end, I found my way to the Provincial Archives on Belleville Street. Here the voices were no longer puzzling. The tapes I listened to carried the same lilting cadences that I'd heard year after year in Winnipeg's North End, except now the voices spoke only Chinese, recalling to my memory the immigrants from decades before. But for me the language barrier remained. So the obstacles to acceptance set in Johnny's path were now added to by obstacles that I, too, could not breach. While some of the Chinese recorded on the tapes did speak in English, their voices lacked the authentic tones of the others — and of Johnny.

A Memorial for Johnny

Then, quite by accident, on a day I had taken off from my search, I was exploring the land about Gonzales Bay, deciding that for the weekend I would become a tourist again, when suddenly there — lying neglected — were a few acres of land that served as a Chinese cemetery. A run-down place, overgrown grass everwhere, although someone had been making an effort to cut it, not with a power lawnmower, but with what must have been a scythe. The gravestones, if I could call them that, were mostly inscribed with Chinese lettering, though some also bore a few recognizable dates. The years of death began somewhere around the turn of the century and reached up through the decades to the thirties, the forties, a rare one or two in the fifties. Others had no dates at all, at least none that I could discern. *Could one of these be Johnny's?* Here is where he would have preferred to be, not freezing to the end of time in the bitter prairie winters, but accepted at last in his own community.

The headstones were not the usual kind — not marble, not polished — but thin slabs of poured concrete, an inch or two thick, a foot wide, and two feet high. And while the cement had been hardening, some ancient scribe had engraved the crucial facts concerning the lives of people about whom more was known in China than could ever be known here. At the foot of one thin concrete slab rested an old pickle jar, with a discolored green label, that housed some red snapdragons. They were tied together by white string and anchored against the wind by a scrap of some wet, crunched-up Chinese newspaper that held the stems in the jar. Nearby, orange silk tiger lilies, flecked with black, lay strewn about on the grass. Toward the back of the cemetery, in the corner furthest from the road, before another concrete slab rested an Island Farm milk carton containing pink and blue plastic carnations. Small flowers of more natural colours — mauves and golds, reds and blues — peeked everywhere from behind stones and weeds.

At last these weary shades rested among their own, drawn to the water's edge, as close to a departure point for their ancient homeland as they had ever managed to get. *Did the water in its murmurings carry secret messages across those ocean currents?* As distant as China was, it was still closer in the dreams of those sleeping figures than this land that, in exchange for allowing them to enter, had turned them into obedient ghosts with such names as Johnny and Petey.

But what now did those sleeping figures dream of? Did the water bear messages, these last few weeks, of tanks crushing students in Tiananmen Square, of cries ringing out amid rifle fire, of dissenting soldiers executed while the youth of China was trampled upon by a fierce, red-eyed dragon that could still breathe fire? Or did their dreams mingle instead with those of the terra cotta warriors buried now for twenty-one centuries in Shaanxi Province? Were Johnny and the others lying there still part of an ancient China that had demanded — and received — an obedience so strong it survived even after death?

Out of such conjectures, how can I write a story about Johnny and those other wandering figures who had made their way across the ocean so many decades before? I don't even know what his real name is. Let's call him Chung Lee Wong.

When I first knew him, he had been separated from his wife and children for almost thirty years and yet he

A Memorial for Johnny

was still determined to get them out of China. *And where in China did he come from?* Let's say — as I have already recorded and I think I remember correctly — from Kirin Province, from the town of Yantsi.

He came here about *1912*, right? Shortly before World War I. Not long after the Emperor had been overthrown, the Ch'ing Dynasty had fallen, and Johnny's father — to signal the end of his servitude — had cut off his pigtail. Johnny had expected to send for his wife and children in a year or two, but the war intervened. He lived in Victoria those first few months in a house where rooms were divided by bunkbeds into cubicles about ten feet square. In the bed directly above him was a fellow Chinese immigrant who'd been on the same boat coming to Canada. For this room with no view to speak of, he paid $4.00 a month.

He remained in Victoria only three months, working first in a vegetable store, then at a restaurant, and finally in a Chinese laundry. He was fired from the vegetable store because of some mistakes in handling the unfamiliar currency, currency imprinted with the faces of monarchs that demanded from him — pigtail or no pigtail — instant recognition. The restaurant job ended when he somehow managed to spill a single plate of soup on an entire table of guests — immigration officials — from Ottawa, on the final stage of a fact-finding tour. And the laundry job did not survive long after he burned an iron imprint into a pretty green and yellow dress belonging to a local councillor's wife.

Feelings had grown so violent against him, in just those three months, that soon rumours were circulating up and down the streets and in the alleyways that one of these nights he would be flung back on a freighter leaving for China. When the voices reached a certain hysterical pitch, he thought it best to set off by foot for Nanaimo one night rather than risk returning to his cubicle after yet another terrifying day at work.

He had not been on the road for much more than an hour when a car filled with miners working at the Dunsmuir Pits stopped on their way back from Victoria to pick him up. "Sure, Johnny, there's lots of work in Nanaimo," they assured him, and suddenly he had a new Canadian identity and a new job. "It terrible job! You no believe!" he told me. "Work from four in morning to nine at night. And all time smell of oil everywhere. Use fish oil for lamps. Must see to work in tunnels. Bodies steam just like mules and horses down in mine. Heads rub raw bumping on low roofs. Thirty-five cents gallon, oil cost. Buy drums — 45 gallon — from Indians. Indians make oil from fish liver. Johnny want secret recipe for oil. But Indians laugh, because secret keep Indians fishing on water, in sunlight, able to see mountains, not swinging pickaxe in dark like Johnny for $2.00 a day. Some days Johnny shovel tons and tons of coal onto rail car. But not when Johnny hear buzzing sound. Then turn down lantern — quick! Buzzing sound is gas bubbling out of water in tunnel walls. Johnny back up. Work in other tunnel. Wait for weeks; maybe go back with others. Then explosions. Every two, three months — more explosions. But coal — Dunsmuir Coal — best in world. Take to bunkhouse all Johnny want. Burn easy, clean — like cigar.

"But then others get mad. 'More money', they say. We strike. And Colonel Villiers, owner of mine, he get mad too. He live in big white house — by bay. He own two dogs — big, big mastiffs. Mikey and Nero. Colonel Villier, he wear uniform, leather boots, and come to meeting. He say all Chinese be sent back to China. White miners, too, if he have his way. He give not penny more. He say grass will grow on streets of Nanaimo — he will see it. He make vow. But no more money. No. He say, before he leave, water from bay will flow like river in streets of town."

Johnny had probably decided that this was as good a time as any to leave — and probably better than most. He wasn't going to wait till some troops came round, as Colonel Villier threatened, to bully him onto a boat with hundreds of others for the return trip to China. Canada had not been what he expected, he told me: "Lose work in vegetable store, in restaurant, in laundry, then lucky and keep job in mine, with explosions, fish oil, steaming horses, mules, gas bubbling through water." But he was stubborn. He had heard that somewhere in North America — for sure down East, maybe in Ontario — was a gold mountain and he was determined first to find it and then mine it.

So one night, after listening to Colonel Villier threaten once more that he would shut the mine down altogether, Johnny caught the ferry for the mainland. The next day he joined a work crew with the railroad that was helping to build a track to a coal mine in the interior of BC Again the pay was $2.00 a day. I see him in some obscure mountain pass with a sledge hammer raised over his head. A treacherous pass: thirty men died in a rock slide the day before Johnny arrived.

Others claim to have driven the last spike in the line through Eagle Pass in 1885. But it was Johnny, in 1913 — laboring in the heat, black flies swarming about him, sleeping in a shed outside of which bears (perhaps even a grizzly) prowled about in the darkness — who worked on another line, never recorded, never acknowledged or celebrated, for almost a year. And it was Johnny, for sure, who drove the last spike in that line. After that he was driven off by some second-generation Canadians who set fire to his sleeping shack. They had, it seems, listened only too well to the words of Mackenzie King back in 1908, when he was Deputy Minister of Labor: "That Canada should desire to restrict immigration from the Orient is . . . natural," he insisted in those carefully measured tones that transmitted sentiments from the spirit world with the same accuracy. "Canada should remain a white man's country."

Then it was eastward to Ontario, to Marathon — a journey which took him four years: from 1914 to 1918. *Was he even aware of World War I?* Probably. It would have made it easier for him to get jobs: delivering groceries in Lethbridge, sweeping the streets in Moose Jaw, washing dishes in Brandon. He was too much of a nonentity, too thin and small of stature, to be noticed or pressured into enlisting, even if he could have found the recruiting office. No blonde, blue-eyed beauty was going to disarm him with an inviting smile, then saunter coyly up, only to put a white feather in his lapel. The Battle of the Somme, Vimy Ridge, Passchendaele — all would have been as indecipherable to him as his marks on our laundry parcels were to us, even though they bore our names. So much chatter on the radio, black headlines in the papers, cheering crowds at war's end while he peeled potatoes, swept

A Memorial for Johnny

floors, emptied garbage cans. Until at last he arrived in Marathon.

As soon as he got off the train, he began looking about for work at the nearest Chinese laundry. But a Chinese laundry was still beyond Marathon's means. So he settled instead for a job as a cook in a restaurant. *Where had he trained as a cook? Who taught him?* It is a given: he was a cook. Never mind where he trained. Perhaps he learned while working in the interior of BC There the food had been so awful that he had taken to cooking for the other Chinese on the gang, and they preferred his northern China dishes. He had a natural bent for cooking. *But why did his talent take this direction?* You ask too many questions. He may never have been a cook before, maybe not even have been one of a gang of coolies working for the CPR All that is known for certain is what I knew about him when he was about fifty, had a wife and family, a boy and an older girl. Johnny had been married for five years before he signed up to go to Canada. He nearly died on the way over. *Really?* Who knows? Let's *say* he had a queasy stomach. He shared a two-man cabin with eight other Chinese. The Black Hole of Calcutta was the Hilton by comparison with what he put up with. But he endured, survived. He also learned to bake pies — somewhere. Then it was on to Marathon, where he spent the next half-dozen years.

Immigrant trains were steaming through every day, filled with people who'd been stowed below decks on packed boats coming from Eastern Europe. My father was on one that stopped at Marathon. Yes, I'm sure he stopped in Marathon, Ontario, in 1924. So there they were — immigrants from opposite hemispheres, meeting in Marathon.

And my mother, to whom he sent a Cunard boat ticket, came through one year later.

And what did Johnny do? Why he provided meals — superb meals that made the passengers ignore the over-priced, inedible fare that never would have passed anywhere else in the world as food, but that the CPR packaged in boxes and had the immigrants sign a chit for.

His specialty was not chop suey, but — let us say — beef stew. Yes. With lots of carrots, onions and potatoes in the thick gravy. The bread he baked himself. Along with the blueberry and apple and raspberry pies. These were the *pièces de résistance*, for those who could afford them. Nothing could match his pies. The immigrants' eyes lit up when they tasted the first bite. Yet in Marathon, where his presence certainly did not add a touch of cosmopolitan flavour to the town, he was barely tolerated. Here again he slept in a shack till it was burned down by other residents of Marathon, who if they didn't take their cue from Mackenzie King must have been still mesmerized by the words of John A. Macdonald back in 1885. It was the year Chinese labourers had helped complete the CPR, and Macdonald felt the occasion should not pass without some appropriate words to commemorate that achievement: "The Chinese immigrant has no common interest with us . . . and is valuable, the same as a threshing machine . . . He has no British instincts or British feeling and therefore ought not to have a vote."

I am only now piecing together certain conjectures — certain possible constructs of our history — from those explorations I have undertaken and from those fragments of the past I have gleaned. Some of them from Johnny's own lips.

Still, Johnny's shack did not get burned down until it was discovered by the restaurant's owner how he got that crisp sugar crust on his pies. When pressed, he would reply, "Johnny no tell. You be mad."

"No, Johnny, no," the bulky proprietress of Auntie Mae's restaurant — a two-hundred-pound woman in her forties — insisted.

"Yes, you be mad."

"Will give you raise, Johnny. Will make you chief cook," Auntie Mae mimicked sweetly. "Everyone knows Johnny's pies are best for thousand miles."

"But Johnny is *only* cook."

"Now, you aren't doubting my word, are you, Johnny?" All the sweetness was gone as she approached menacingly, clenching her big fist in his face.

"Johnny tell! Johnny tell!" he shrieked. "But you no get mad."

"Show me," she insisted.

So Johnny brought a tray of pies to the blazing oven — still ordinary pies at this point — and poured himself some water.

"Now Johnny put sugar into water. So." The white crystals sparkled as they spilled from the spout into the empty marmalade jar that Johnny used for a glass. "And shake." Looking cautiously at the determined owner of the restaurant, Johnny lifted the marmalade jar to his lips and took in a mouthful of the sweetened water, rolling it from cheek to cheek, and then, taking one final look at the round, puzzled face opposite him, blew a fine spray of the mixture over the crusts of the half-dozen pies before him. "Now Johnny put pies in oven, and soon be ready for afternoon train. Now Johnny chief cook in all Marathon. Yes?"

For a moment there was a choking sound in Auntie Mae's throat and her eyes glowered with fury. Then her right arm swung swiftly forward with a blow that caught Johnny on the side of the head and sent him crashing against the pots and pans that hung on the wall.

"Don't stay another minute," she shrieked. "Out! Out! Just get your things and go."

"She one angry lady, that boss lady in Marathon. Very angry!" Johnny insisted.

So maybe it wasn't racism and John A. Macdonald at all that sent that first match blazing so fiercely in the night.

I couldn't help but feel sorry for Johnny because it wasn't hard to guess how he would have felt about it all.

"Then Johnny puzzle. Go to Halifax? But hear *that* town no want more laundries. No want Chinese. Go to Winnipeg? Cold, cold winters. Just like northern China. Johnny decide to wait, see which train come first. At station, see boss lady from restaurant selling pies to people on train from west. Okay, better ride in boxcar back to Winnipeg.

"In Winnipeg, find again old shack. Look just like shack in British Columbia. Like shack in Marathon. So Johnny know it *his* shack. With other Chinese ride in boxcar to Winnipeg — with Petey — open laundry there. Take boards off windows, cut weeds from backyard with scythe and sleep on floor. From owner of shack, learn name of electricity man, Mr. Feldman. He go with Johnny to junkyard and buy there washing machine and old flat irons. Mr. Feldman call it junk, but has garage filled with treasures from everywhere. One Sunday Johnny and Petey carry over tables, chairs, wires, switches, and soon Johnny almost ready for business. It very best shack for Johnny. From grocer Johnny get string and paper — soft, white, no creases, to wrap laundry in. Soft string that break easy. Then go with wagon to each house and ask lady for laundry, and soon Johnny in business. With Petey — for partner. Petey from Toi Shan District in Guangdong Province." *Maybe.*

"After year Johnny bring to Mr. and Mrs. Feldman silk handkerchief that wife send from China. Candy. Fans. Gifts from wife in China."

"Johnny's words recalled another story of those early years, one told to me by my father, Velvel Buchalter. He too, as well as my mother had been the recipient of Johnny's gifts.

"Johnny," my father had asked, "when are you going to have enough money to bring your wife over to Canada? When did you last see her?"

"Johnny no see wife for long time. Fifteen years. Maybe more."

"Fifteen years? Any children?"

"Johnny have one girl, one boy."

Johnny, as my father tells the story, had arrived at their house just before dinner, but my parents were used to his arriving then, and he stood smiling in the kitchen doorway. "How old are your children, Johnny?"

"Children maybe so tall," Johnny indicated with a hand to his forehead, then to his shoulder.

"They must be almost grown up by now," said my father.

"Yes, soon — in few years — they marry. Johnny no see."

My father had been upset. "How much money do they need for tickets, Johnny?"

"For tickets?"

"Boat tickets to come to Canada."

"Johnny have money. Save from railroad and restaurant. But no can bring. Pay even head tax. But no can bring. Not allowed."

"Sit down, Johnny. I'll get you a bowl of soup. Chicken soup with *mondloch*," my mother said. "But first we have to bless the candles."

Johnny, my father had thought, watched with curiosity as the candles were lit and blessed. Perhaps he would have liked to light some candles of his own, just on speculation.

The next week when he brought back the laundry, he also brought along a blueberry pie. But all my mother's cajoling to learn how he got the crust so crisp and tasty could not coax the secret from him.

So Johnny went on washing laundry and baking pies through the next few years — years that saw my brother's arrival on the scene and then my own, years that began turning into decades. Then one fall in 1948 the papers were filled with news of Mao Tse-tung's sweep from northern China down towards Peking. Chiang Kai-shek was preparing to flee to Formosa. Massive weapon shipments were sent by America to the Nationalist forces, but they were promptly sold off to the Communists by corrupt officials. Down into southern China Mao Tse-tung swept.

A Memorial for Johnny

I remember because I was sixteen years old and I saw it on the Movie Tone News. Instinctively, I sensed danger to Johnny's wife and children. Three years earlier, I recalled, the Movie Tone News had blazed with scenes from another war, and there were the camps in Germany and Poland full of the ashes that had once been human lives.

"Johnny, what do you think of the changes in China?" my father asked one evening when Johnny had returned with several parcels wrapped in that soft, white paper and had taken what had become his accustomed seat in the chair beside mine at one end of the table.

"Yes, new boss in China now." Johnny sipped his chicken soup thoughtfully.

"Are you from North or South China?"

"Johnny not from North." Then, more emphatically between sips of chicken soup, "No."

"I thought you were from the North, Johnny," I interrupted. "Be quiet, Michael," my father frowned.

"No, Johnny not Communist."

"But what will happen now? With your wife? Your children?"

"Johnny get letter from wife in spring." And he drew from his grey corduroy jacket pocket the letter with large colorful stamps. The pages seemed as soft and fragile as the paper he used in the laundry. He gave the envelope and pages to my father, who passed them on to my mother and eventually they came to my brother and me. Pages filled with mysterious strokes and dots — a Morse code we would never decipher, though what the letter meant was all too clear to Johnny.

"She try to get on boat. Last year — December."

"Have you heard of anything since then, Johnny?"

"Long time — nothing. Maybe soon." And he smiled again and was gone.

The next Friday we were going early to my grandparents for the Sabbath supper so I was sent to pick up the laundry that was to have been delivered later that day.

"Not ready yet," Johnny insisted. "But soon."

"Have you heard yet from your wife?" I asked. Johnny was laying out a shirt on the ironing board. He seemed not to have heard me — or did not want to hear me. From behind him, he reached for a fly sprayer whose glass container was filled with water and whose handle had been removed. Johnny slipped the metal tube between his lips and filled his cheeks with air. Then a fine mist was blown over the shirt. Deftly the flat iron smoothed the wrinkles from the collar, sleeves, back and then front. Again the process was repeated. And again. Finally all the laundry was ready, wrapped and neatly tied with string. "See, Johnny's mark," and then he drew, with several deft strokes, the Chinese characters for his name and for ours. *Did he ever write to his wife about us? Were the Feldman's spoken of back in China? Were we listed in some Communist commissar's records? Were our Sabbath candles puzzled over? And how was Johnny viewed there? As a wealthy shop owner and successful businessman? Would his family have dared relate the episodes of his life?*

As I was about to leave, Johnny reached for the usual blueberry pie, still warm from the oven. "Johnny once bake pies for trains." He watched my face closely as he went on to tell the story of his period of glory as Marathon's Master Baker of Pies. "But no tell Mama," he insisted. And from that day to this, I've never told a soul.

A Memorial for Johnny

A few years later I was off to university in Toronto, and when I next returned to Selkirk Avenue, I noticed several changes on the block. The shoemaker's shop which had been little more than a hovel at Selkirk and Charles was gone, replaced by a modern brick drugstore. Across the street the grocery store had been boarded up, the building condemned. Soon, I expected, it would be seized by the city and torn down altogether. *And where was Johnny's laundry that had been next to the Catholic church?* For years I had listened to Johnny and Petey chatting to each other in their shop — those high-pitched voices rising and tinkling together, their sounds as indecipherable to me as the chants that rang and chimed from the Holy Ghost Church next door. Now the laundry had been torn down and replaced by a motorcycle shop. The showroom glittered with the appearance of power and wealth: shiny chrome handlebars, gleaming black bodies with bright exhausts that could trumpet rooty-toot-toot in defiance, and leather saddlebags whose borders were lined with the polished brass heads of rivets. All signs of the naked lightbulbs, the flat irons, the old ruin of a cast-iron boiler, the wooden-drum washer, wiring tacked to the outside of cracking plaster, calendars used for record books, and rolls of soft, white paper — all must have been bulldozed months ago into giant trucks and trundled off into oblivion.

But I had underestimated Johnny. My mother told me he'd found another shack on Main Street near the Redwood Bridge — next to Zimmerman the glazier. It was too far for him to bring us the laundry now. But when I entered, Johnny was behind the counter just as he used to be, and there — still operating — were the washer and flat irons, and there, too, was that fly sprayer and still naked lightbulb. Near the entrance hung a photograph of the former laundry on Selkirk Avenue — a lopsided, unpainted structure, windows without curtains, the top of the chimney missing a few bricks. The black and white photo showed Johnny and Petey smiling proudly from the doorway.

When the laundry was bundled up, the gift of yet another blueberry pie was accompanied by the usual reminder, "Remember, no tell Mama about pie crust," he insisted as we shook hands. The skin felt soft, supple, fragile, as though it might tear if I pressed it too tightly.

It was a test of my loyalty, I knew. "I wouldn't dare," I laughed.

"Wait! Johnny have more gift for you." And he vanished behind the stairs to a back room and returned with a silk handkerchief: oranges and reds and yellows turned and twisted into dragon shapes breathing fire. Soft delicate material alive with explosive energy.

"You take."

Years later, long after Johnny had vanished — for good this time, I feared — a feature article with many pictures appeared in an inner section of the *Winnipeg Free Press*:

CHINESE LAUNDRY PRESERVED IN NATIONAL MUSEUM
LAUNDRY EQUIPMENT SHIPPED TO OTTAWA
WHOLE ERA ENDS

But where was Johnny? Was he not even to be remembered among the artifacts? — always to be ignored? Was that his fate? To be recalled only by those companions in

A Memorial for Johnny

that crowded boat cabin for whom the passage to Canada would be the experience of a lifetime? To be remembered only by those fellow coolies who laboured at some railway pass and were sustained by Johnny's cooking? Or only by immigrants, on trains passing through Marathon, purchasing pies with unforgettable crusts? Pies passed up to train windows as immigrants gazed bewilderedly into a land that looked, despite its vastness — or perhaps because of it — as if it might not be so inviting after all.

And so, decades later, I had taken the opportunity of a sabbatical year and sought out Johnny in the only place left to look: among the records housed in Asian House in Vancouver. *When would he have come over? Were there immigration waves from China? From which province? How long would they have labored on the CPR lines? What became of them afterward?*

The Chinese girl I spoke to was so striking in appearance — so memorable, a bright flower not at all ready to vanish into oblivion as Johnny had.

"What was his Chinese name?" she asked. "How old was he?" Did I know the name of his Chinese partner in the laundry in Winnipeg? What kind of design had been on the silk scarf he gave me? Could I describe it? Why did I want to find him? I could see she was puzzled by my interest. Who was this stranger inquiring about some Chinese laundryman? Didn't I know the Chinese no longer ran neighbourhood laundries? Did she suspect that I would produce a bag of dirty clothes and ask her if I could leave them there to be washed and ironed? Did I really think she'd have some of that soft, white paper and weak string to wrap them into a bundle?

"There are other stories, happier stories that can be told," she insisted. "Vancouver has many successful, many important Chinese who might agree to an interview. We are very proud of our recent immigrants from Hong Kong."

So there were no answers to be found here, and I left feeling very much like Johnny as I tramped the streets through Chinatown in Vancouver. That girl back in Asian House, I wondered, she was easily old enough to be Johnny's granddaughter. She must know what Johnny would have been like. Did she or her friends not have a grandparent like Johnny? I wanted to break down all official barriers. I wanted to say to her, "I knew your grandfather. He told me all about you. Can you not tell me anything about him?"

Instead, like Johnny, I take to my table some sheets of soft, white paper. *These marks, are they more decipherable now? Can they tell his story? Do they present clearly, cleanly, the one who wandered across an ocean and across a land, and who continued — all those years — to be more than a ghost, yet not quite a fully recognizable human being?* The memories of Johnny will some day have to be sorted out and laundered, cleansed of misconceptions, properly wrapped, passed on, and eventually looked at and tried on in the light of day. Till then, these fragments of memories and conjectures must stand. Like some faded red and blue flowers wrapped in paper, they are perhaps the only memorial that Johnny will ever have. So I conclude his story and read his name now aloud, as if from a barely decipherable tombstone:

Chung Lee Wong (?)
Born: 1890 (?) Yantsi, Province of Kirin (?)
Died: 1957 (?) Victoria, BC (?)

A Memorial for Johnny

Note:
The epigraph is translated from a poem scratched into the brick wall of his cell by a Chinese immigrant confined in the Immigration Building in Victoria in the early 1900's. He was either ill or unable to pay the head tax of $500 and was awaiting deportation back to China.

Lucifer in Starlight

When David phoned to say that he and Ruthie would be flying down here for Alvin's bar mitzvah, I couldn't believe it. Marsha hadn't heard from her brother and sister-in-law in years, and I'd told her she'd just be upset if she sent out an invitation and they didn't come. But no, like always she had to have her way. Keeping up appearances is part of her family's tradition.

David's become a Canadian — a hot-shot English professor at a university in Winnipeg. In the summer break, he usually gets a research grant to jet off to London, Paris or Rome. So what would be the big attraction, anyway, to come out to this God-forsaken place?

But as soon as I picked up the phone and heard his voice, I knew we'd been wrong. "Sorry," I told him. "Not a chance I'll be able to pick you up at the airport. I've got deliveries every week to places as far away as Fresno and Monterey, and that's a lot of driving, year in, year out." But David said not to worry. When he and Ruthie arrived on Wednesday, they'd rent an Oldsmobile in LA, stay at the downtown Hilton, and look around for a couple of days. Then, on Friday, drive up here for Alvin's bar mitzvah. It would be a short visit — three days at most. Okay, I thought, if you want to throw away good money with both hands, that's your business. But don't expect me to be impressed. Never had a bar mitzvah myself, and the more the relatives screamed, the more I knew I wasn't missing out on much. But there is no stopping Marsha.

We've had to work pretty hard to make a go of things here. Ten acres — all fenced — and every year we sell about thirty thousand rabbits. Maybe a few thousand more in good years. We got hutches built everywhere and planted trees for shade. And there's a huge fenced-in garden. Really desert, you know, but the makeshift irrigation system just manages to hold its own. Except when the wind starts blowing in through the gulches. Then the heat hits you like a blowtorch. Early morning's alright, though. You can go off for a walk in the hills and not meet anyone except a coyote or two. That's two things you got to watch out for around here — coyotes and hawks. One morning I was coming back from a walk and, so help me, there were two hawks tearing at the chicken wire, trying to get into the hutches at those rabbits. And then there are the snakes. Sure do have our hands full around here — getting 500-600 rabbits ready each week to truck out. And when the coyotes and hawks and snakes have their minds made up to get their fair share, damned if they don't.

That's why our house isn't finished. Oh, the roof's on alright and the windows are all in, but most of the wall panelling inside is still just tacked on to the framing. We'd be okay if it weren't for that damn mortgage. Why, the whole place must be worth a quarter million, though it doesn't look it. We don't look it either in these *goyish* work clothes we get from the war surplus store in Bakersfield.

Now we're going to have to get all spruced up for Alvin's bar mitzvah. I don't know why Alvin needed a bar mitzvah anyway, but Marsha said he did. Same as she said we had to take in those two stray mutts: part German shepherd and part God-knows-what. Mind you, Jess and Boon do make it pretty rough on any coyote comes sneaking in here. They're clever, too, won't get lured off and ambushed in the hills. Problem is, though, Boon doesn't get along with our goat Lucifer. But I'm kind of fond of Lucifer, and he doesn't cost us a penny. Any scrap of lettuce and carrots the rabbits won't touch, Lucifer takes care of.

Well, on Friday morning, there was Marsha in a dress of all things. Ever since we got married and bought the ranch she's been wearing army fatigues for work, or else blue jeans and plaid shirts if we go out. Didn't even know she had any other clothes around anymore. And she had Alvin all spruced up too: dress trousers, and a new shirt, tie and jacket she'd bought at Sear's Roebuck. Had to cost something.

About noon, David and Ruthie pulled up into the yard in a shiny mauve Oldsmobile. Just to rent it must have set them back quite a bit. Would've taken me almost a hundred rabbits to earn that kind of money.

As soon as Marsha sees David getting out of the car in the yard, she comes racing out of the house and hangs onto him for dear life. As if he were her *saviour* or something. I couldn't believe my eyes.

It's true, I wouldn't have minded giving Ruthie a big hug myself — she's a sleek and silky-looking gal — but at the last minute she turns her head and kind of gives me a glance that says a peck on the cheek is enough.

Ruthie seemed put out with the house being only half finished: naked bulbs hanging from the ceiling, no doors on the rooms, a plastic pipe leading outside from the kitchen sink, and no bannister on the stairs. But Marsha had put some rose drapes over the doorway to the guest room and I could see Ruthie looked pleased. So she can look pleased about some things.

"I've got dinner ready," Marsha called. And we all went into the kitchen. That Marsha, she can still surprise you. Trouble is she goes overboard. Here she'd gone and bought a couple of bottles of wine, two dozen ears of corn, three frying chickens, and, for dessert, a cherry pie. Sure knows how to waste money alright. After all, what does she think we raise rabbits for? Everyone says they taste just like chicken. And she knows as well as I do where we could have gotten some fruit to bake a pie — absolutely free. And the wine, too, most likely. But I could see from the way she kept watching her brother all through the meal and squeezing his hand that what really mattered to her now was having him here.

"Remember the last time we were in California together, David?"

"Of course, I remember. It was during the Depression. When you were seven and I was nine."

"And Uncle Herbie had written how this fruit farm he had was the Promised Land, and he sent Mom and Pop the bus tickets from New York to California?"

"That was some ride, Marsha. It took a full week. But we never got tired of looking out the windows. It was like a movie — a travelogue — but not in black and white. In full color. And we were going to be in it."

"We would have made it sooner, but Pop got alarmed when he saw how far we were getting from New York, and we stopped off in Illinois for a day till Mom was able to argue him back onto the bus."

"Then there were those grain fields stretching out to the horizon and farm houses nestled in among clusters of trees."

"And somewhere along the way there was a derelict barn that had been pushed way over by the wind. It looked as if it had been falling over for the last dozen years."

"What I remember, Martha, are all those cattle grazing behind barbed wire fences that stretched for miles. Till we got to the desert. But beyond the desert were the fruit farms and neat rows of vineyards that climbed the sky. Sprinklers everywhere and men labouring behind barbed wire fences."

"Don't forget those 'No Trespassing' signs with the dark outline of a shotgun above the printing."

"And after all that, when we got to Uncle Herbie's we stayed two weeks and Pop said he couldn't stand it — it was all just too lush for him — and he browbeat Uncle Herbie into giving us the money to go back. Threatened to take him to court."

"Then why'd we come in the first place, David?"

"Because we were evicted from our apartment. In a new place, the first month was always free, and then, when we couldn't pay the rent, it would take the landlord another month before he could get us out. We'd been moving every two months for years. Mom wanted a place where we could stay put for awhile, and so when Uncle Herbie offered to pay for us to come out here, she jumped at the chance."

"So why didn't Pop like California?"

"He just got to feeling uncomfortable without hard pavement under his feet and the smell of exhaust in the air. When he looked up he expected to see skyscrapers, not trees. Don't forget he'd spent his whole life distributing flyers and selling umbrellas in Manhattan."

I could see Alvin was drinking all this in along with his glass of wine, and I knew if I wasn't careful, next thing I knew he'd be wanting to take a bus trip to New York himself.

"Tell me about the Pants Gang," he demanded. "Mom says they were robbers, but that's all she can remember."

"They were a gang of robbers who stole from stores in the South Bronx."

"What kind of stores?"

"Any store that had a cash register."

"But why were they called the Pants Gang?"

"Because after they robbed a store, they made everyone take off their pants and lie on the floor. So when the gang ran off down the street, no one would chase after them."

"They didn't have a getaway car?"

"Who could afford a car?"

After dinner I showed David and Ruthie around the ranch, and I could see they were surprised at how many rabbits we had. "This place could sell for close to a quarter million," I let them know. "But the mortgage payments grind us down and we've been kept so busy that it looks more like a hand-to-mouth operation. Haven't had a moment to fix up the house, though Marsha keeps getting after me to finish it. But there's always something to watch out for."

"What sort of things?" David looked puzzled.

"Well, like last month there was a wind came tearing out of the desert so fierce it ripped the shingles off the roof. But worse still, it knocked some of my rabbit hutches over — and part of the wire fence. Lost over three hundred rabbits that night."

"Where'd they run off to?"

"Off into the hills, I guess."

"Could they survive out there?" asked Ruthie.

"Well, there isn't a whole lot of vegetation for them to eat, and the sun does blaze something fierce. But if they could survive those dry desert winds, with no rain, why all they'd have to face would be the snakes and coyotes and hawks."

"Oh, no," said Ruthie, "they would all have died. That's terrible."

"Look," I said, "would you like to see Jess's litter of pups? Arrived just last night. They're in the shed, back of the house." Right away Ruthie brightened up.

Lucifer was hanging around back there and I could hear Jess growling, warning him to stay out.

"Oh, no you don't," I said, and tried to give him a good, swift kick. But without much luck. For the moment, though, he was gone.

"Don't they get along?" Ruthie asked.

"Not at all. And with good reason."

She looked at me as if to ask why, but no, I told myself, better not tell her.

"Would you like to hold one of the pups?" I asked, and when she nodded, I chose the pick of the litter: a darkish-brown little guy with white markings on his paws and muzzle. Jess was pretty good, too; even let Ruthie pat her with scarcely a growl. But when I actually went to give Ruthie the pup, Jess was up on her feet like a flash. "Better not," I said. "She's kind of high-strung now," and I put the pup down with the others.

"Is there something wrong with one of them?" Ruthie asked. "The one that's asleep looks smaller than the others."

"Can't tell yet. We'll see."

"What do you do with so many puppies?"

"I put a sign up on the road and they'll all be spoken for in a week."

"Oh, that's a relief."

I could see what she'd been thinking, so I told her, "No, nothing gets wasted here."

When we got back to the house, we could see Lucifer peering round from the front, but then Boon caught sight of him and they were off. That goat got chased every which way, back and forth between the rabbit hutches, round and round the house and vegetable garden, even over a barbed wire fence and then towards the dried-out riverbed a quarter mile away. But you could see Lucifer was scared as the devil to end up there, and he tore first this way and then that, determined to get back to the ranch, and lucky he did too. Those coyotes would make short work of him if he ever got cut off from the house.

God, we laughed at all their clowning, though, all that barking and leaping up into the air. The rabbits came running out of their hutches to see what all the commotion was about. At first, I thought they'd come out to enjoy the show, but the next thing I knew they were racing back and forth with fright, trying to tear their way past the wire netting. Dumb rabbits. Wouldn't have lasted till nightfall if they'd gotten out. A miniature cyclone they were. Or a three-ring circus. But they did add to the fun.

That Ruthie — she sure can laugh. David, too. Not stuffy at all. Kind of broke the ice, that show the animals put on.

"Do they often tear around like that?"

"Whenever the notion takes them. Lucifer's gotten pretty good at not getting driven out into the desert, and Boon's gotten pretty good at making it all but impossible for him to get back here. They're a real comedy team, those two."

For supper, David offered to take us all to a restaurant. The only trouble was all the fancy ones are in Bakersfield and on a Friday night you need a reservation for any one of them. So we settled instead for Smitty's: hamburgers, hotdogs, pancakes, that sort of thing. But still Marsha insisted we get all spruced up, just as if we were going to the Ritz. We got there about eight and right away I felt this is our night. There was a crowd, and we had to go right to the back of the place to find a table.

All through the meal, Marsha kept looking at her brother, hanging on his every word, so she didn't see what I was up to. And Alvin was still thinking about our conversation earlier in the afternoon.

"Uncle David, was Zeyda glad when you all got back to New York?"

"All the way back across America, he kept talking about how happy he would be. Even when we got stuck in Kansas City because we ran out of money and he actually went out on the street and panhandled a few dollars so we'd have something to eat the rest of the way back. Your Zeyda — panhandling New York style! 'I'm blind!' he'd call out to whoever came along, staring him straight in the eye, 'and I ain't ate nothin' yet today.' They'd never seen someone as pushy begging for money there, I expect, but that night we were on our way again.

"And you know what your Zeyda did when we got back to New York City?"

"Panhandled some more?"

"No, he was so tired that he almost fell out of the bus. He'd been asleep. And he asked, 'Are we there?'"

"And your Baba at last could say, 'Yes, we're back. Now, where do we sleep tonight?'"

"But he didn't answer. Instead, he listened to the honking and sniffed the exhaust in the air and then he fell down to his knees and kissed the sidewalk."

"Kissed the sidewalk?"

"He'd really felt peculiar out in California. Nothing there seemed real to him."

"And where did you sleep that night?"

"He found a newspaper in a trash can right outside the depot, made a few calls, and in no time at all we were on the subway back into the South Bronx to an apartment where the first month's rent was free if you'd only sign a year's lease."

I could see that even the waiter was interested and kept coming back to the table to listen in. Just so long as he kept his eyes on David and not on me.

At the end of the meal David still hadn't noticed the waiter'd forgotten his fries. I'd just realized it myself. So when he brought along the bill, I said, "Hey, didn't you forget something?"

For a moment he looked blank, and then he got all red in the face. "Sorry about that!"

"Sorry?" I snapped. "You think that makes it right?"

"I'll get you the fries to take out."

"That's more like it."

"Look, if it's all the same to you, Ben, let's forget it. I've had plenty to eat."

And here I'd been working myself up into a temper for him. The waiter felt he was off the hook, but I still didn't think that he should have a three-buck tip. So I slipped back to the table while David was at the cash register and cut it back to fifty cents. Which was about fifty cents too much, anyway, if you ask me.

"Say, what's that clinking sound?" David asked as I settled into the back seat of the Oldsmobile.

"Oh, Ben, you didn't. Not tonight!"

"No one noticed, Marsha. Not even you."

"What did you pocket this time, Dad?"

"First, let's get away from in front of this restaurant." And so by the next set of lights I had everything out on the car floor: salt and pepper shakers, two sets of cutlery, sugar bowl, matches, toothpicks, and a huge batch of napkins.

Thought Marsha might be mad or embarrassed. But when she realized I'd gotten so much stuff she just couldn't help laughing. And then David and Ruthie joined in, too. David said how his Pop in New York would have gotten a kick out of it all. Seeing as how well they were taking it, I thought, hell, why not go the whole hog?

"Let's stop for a few minutes at the Safeway before we head back to the ranch. It's on the way."

"Ben! No! Absolutely not!"

"Oh, Mom! Don't be a spoilsport."

"I'll just be a few minutes. The store should be shut by now."

David was puzzled, I could see, but we had to go by the Safeway anyway, so he slowed down as we drove past. "You're right. The store must be shut," he said. "You can see the place is deserted."

"Good. Now if you could just drive us around the back, by the shipping dock, this shouldn't take long at all."

David turned to look at me, more puzzled than ever, but then swung the car around. And boy, was he ever surprised. Every man and his dog were there with pickup trucks, wagons, bicycles, anything on wheels. It was a real sideshow, no doubt about it.

"Now if you'll just open the trunk, David," I called as I slipped out the back door. Alvin was right behind me and in a moment we were up on the shipping dock scrambling with all the others. First, I went for the boxes and right away I hit the jackpot. One was soaked with spilled wine, but when I opened the case I saw that only a couple of bottles were broken: the rest had just been waiting for us. "They don't care," I explained to David. "If there's any sign of spillage, the shipping clerks dump the whole case. It's easier."

By then David had got the idea, and he pitched right in. His Pop would have been proud. Right away he spotted a box of oranges that had a few mouldy ones packed in with the rest. I grabbed whole boxes crammed with spoiled lettuce and carrots, or with bunches of turnips and beets that had wilted tops.

"What you want those for?" someone else who'd worked himself into a lather asked. "They're not fit for eating!"

"Not for you or me, maybe, but my rabbits think it's a feast. And what the rabbits won't touch, the goat'll take care of."

By now we were all working at top speed racing around the dock or reaching over to check out what was in the huge metal garbage bins. And every once in a while, the clerks who were working overtime in the receiving area would dump out some more produce.

All of a sudden the door opened and a huge box got shoved out. Quick as a flash, five families were racing for it, but Alvin was there first and kicked it off the dock to David, who dumped it in the back seat. "Good boy," I called out. "That'll be all the stale bread and buns and cakes."

Boy, were we ever in a frenzy by then. It was like sharks at feeding time. Really fierce looks were coming our way as we snaffled leaking quarts of milk, cartons of eggs with one or two broken ones, laundry detergent in wet boxes, and badly dented tins of soft drinks with just a few leaking. In less than twenty minutes, I tell you, that shipping dock was clean. One by one the cars and trucks and wagons and bicycle carriers were crammed full, and people started heading off.

"Doesn't this beat going to a movie?" I asked. "And it doesn't cost you anything." Right away, I could see that for David and Ruthie it was a first. "These stores make so much, they can't be bothered sorting through everything.

Doesn't pay for them to have a clerk going through it all. And they don't even have to pay to get all that garbage collected. They just shove it out there on the shipping dock and the next morning there's not a scrap left — at least not if I can help it."

By the time we got back to the ranch it would have been pitch dark outside except for the stars shining real bright. Lucifer was at the car like a shot. I threw him some bunches of turnips and carrots before Boon came charging up and took to chasing him all over the place again. Oh, he's for it now! I thought. But leaping high into the air, Lucifer just managed to escape those snapping teeth before dropping to the ground. And then they were off again. Back of the fence I could see some eyes glowing. Better watch it, Lucifer. You get chased out into the desert and those coyotes will finish you off faster than we cleared off that shipping dock.

It took no more than fifteen minutes with all of us helping to empty out the car. I wondered what Hertz would do, though, when that posh Oldsmobile was returned smelling like a garbage can. Then we went into the kitchen and Marsha brewed up fresh coffee and served up some more cherry pie and ice cream.

Afterwards I was thinking it wasn't so bad with David and Ruthie visiting. They sure weren't stuffy like I thought. They'd pitched right in and helped. Just goes to show how wrong you can be. No, they're not stuffy at all. It was just the other way around.

The trouble started early the next morning when we were getting ready to go into Bakersfield for Alvin's bar mitzvah. Agnes, who often helps out at a fruit farm down the way, had dropped by to see Jess's new litter of pups, and right away she spots the one who looks pretty tiny now compared to the rest. At once she raises a fuss and the next thing I know Ruthie's joined in, too. So what do they do but get David to drive off down the highway and come back with a baby bottle, of all things. And in no time, they've coaxed Jess into letting them try to feed it. They were all back there trying to help, Marsha and Alvin and the rest, but as soon as I saw what they were up to I told them it was a waste of time. But no, they had to have their way. Ruthie kept trying to give the runt a bottle, except it kept choking and spitting it all back out. She even warmed the milk and put sugar in it.

Finally, I said, "Well, we can hang around here wasting our time forever or we can drive out to Bakersfield for what we've all gotten ready for in the first place." So we all piled into the Oldsmobile, but only after Ruthie had shown Agnes how to hold the pup and try to give it the warm, sweet milk. Of course, I'd known all along it wasn't going to work out. And just as we were getting into the car, it happened.

I guess Agnes kept giving the little guy more milk than he could swallow and finally he must have been nearly drowning. For such a tiny thing he really did let out a yell. Sounded like a baby screaming. Right away Ruthie got out of the car to see if she could help. Then she was back — all white-faced — and we were off.

"Now I'm not all that stuck on this bar mitzvah stuff myself," I told David, "but I figure if you're going to go ahead with it, you might as well be there from the beginning." So David got that Oldsmobile really rocketing along, and I was just starting to relax when Ruthie snapped at me, "You don't really care, do you, if that little pup lives or dies?"

I looked back into those hard, flashing eyes and thought, Dammit all, anyway! But she just kept staring at me, and so finally I said, "I guess if you were at the ranch all the time, you'd not be carrying on so." And then I had a sudden hunch and said, "Haven't you ever given away a pet cat or dog to the Humane Society? They can't find homes for all of them, you know." And right away I could see I'd touched home.

The synagogue in Bakersfield is an old place and smells kind of dusty. But it was pretty well packed with all these older men in conservative suits and the women in their finest dresses bought especially for *shiel*. They really knew their stuff, too, flipping pages like mad, carrying the Torah through the aisles, then having Alvin come up to the table in front of the ark to take over the service and read the *Maftir*. And there was that silver metal pointer moving across the parchment, and in those voices I heard the names of Abraham, Isaac and Jacob being chanted. After a while I could see how, if a person could half follow it, this chanting and praying could take on a life of its own. Like a swarm of bees in a hive — all humming away, all golden — with a crown flashing on top of the rolled-up Torah now, and the cantor's voice starting off deep and taking the rest of the congregation with him. But then it turned into something else — with the voices telling of a people lost in the desert and almost vanishing altogether. Then everything changed again, and suddenly we were back to those golden sounds, those prayers intermingled with *Hallelujahs!*

Alvin's teacher was really pleased with how everything was going. And after Alvin had his turn at carrying the Torah around the aisles and it was safely back in the ark, the people sitting in the balcony rained down candy on him, and on us, and on the rabbi and cantor, and on the ark itself. And then it was over and Marsha, I could tell, was real happy — happier than she'd been in years, and Alvin looked more than usually pleased with himself.

Afterward, in the lobby, we had some whiskey and coffee and honey cake. Everyone came over to congratulate Alvin, Marsha and even me. And I hadn't even wanted all this. So we were feeling kind of good by the time we left, and I said maybe we should stop for lunch at a restaurant, but Marsha said no, and Ruthie stared at me as if to say enough is enough. It wasn't funny anymore. Just when I was beginning to get on with them, too.

So it was back in silence to the ranch and, sure enough, David drove right up to the shed where Jess and her pups were. The pup just lay there on a piece of old sacking, and the empty bottle lay beside it. Milk was all over its face and chest. Not even Jess seemed to care anymore, and the other pups now looked about twice its size. Ruthie picked it up and ran her finger along its back and stroked its face, but nothing was going to help now.

Agnes came over with her eyes red and her mouth all screwed up. "I tried and tried. But after you left in the car, I couldn't do anything with him."

Ruthie didn't seem to have heard a word. I looked at her and wondered, what is she thinking about, all so white-faced again? And then I realized she wasn't just thinking about what was happening now. She was still hearing that long scream from before.

Kind of dampened everything down after the celebration in Bakersfield. David said they'd have to be packing up their suitcases now for the long drive back to LA first thing in the morning. As they all drifted back into the house, I thought, dammit, I was right. They should never have come.

I went over to the shed again and picked up the dead pup. Didn't look cute at all now. Walked over to the fence and thought, what am I going to do with this thing anyway? I never was one for burying a pet — like it was a human being. Or saying prayers it couldn't even understand. Better not dump it in the garbage just now, though. For all I knew, Ruthie might be watching me from the guestroom window. So I kept walking around the house till the only bedroom window facing me was mine and Marsha's.

But what to do with it? Then I felt a familiar nudge from behind, and there was Lucifer. Dependable as sin. Eyes flashing. Sure, why not? Nothing's ever wasted around here. But I found myself putting my hands over my ears to shut out the sounds he was making. And then he was off — jumping over fences, racing back and forth across the yard, leaping triumphantly for stars that wouldn't be out yet for hours. You'd have thought Boon was still after him.

When I went back in, Marsha was standing at our bedroom window staring out. She looked tired. The mood was so heavy I couldn't bear it, and so I went outside and worked among the rabbit hutches by the hour. Time never passed so slowly. It took forever before we got through the rest of the day . . . and the night.

Early the next morning Marsha and Alvin hung around David and Ruthie while they packed up the car. They delayed leaving so long that I thought, I'll bet they're wondering if Marsha and Alvin want to go with them. But then we all said goodbye and at last they were gone. Good, I thought, maybe now I can breathe again. But it wasn't easy.

And it was even harder the following morning. Monday is when Marsha and I start to prepare the rabbits for market, but she hadn't come out yet. Lucifer came nosing around as usual, but somehow I couldn't stomach the sight of him. So I sicced Boon on him. Maybe, I thought, he should be driven out in the desert like his kind used to be. And maybe, just maybe, the hawks or coyotes will get him this time — in fact, I kind of hope they do.

The Hallelujah Girls

The drive from Winnipeg to Arnes takes no more than an hour and a half at the worst of times, but today it felt as if we'd been on the road forever. From the moment, just before breakfast, when Christine had gotten the phone call from Natalie Cooperman, I knew there was going to be trouble. Natalie's husband Larry would be taking out his new sailboat for the first time later that morning. Their elder son, Ross, would be going along as crew. And Natalie wondered if I could be persuaded to come out and offer some pointers, as Larry's knowledge of sailing until now had been derived solely from books.

So Larry was coming out of his printmaking studio into the sunny outdoors. For the weekend, he would be abandoning his copper plates, his inks and acids, his printing press — abandoning a known realm in exchange for one where he was a mere novice.

Now, I have no claim to any great expertise at sailing, but I had managed — just — to stay alive during five summers of boating on Lake Winnipeg. No small achievement, when you consider the treachery that lake is capable of.

It had looked calm when Christine and I set off, but once we passed the power station on the outskirts of the city and the four-lane highway narrowed down to two, the situation changed quickly. From the way the trees were swaying along the highway, I could tell the wind would be an offshore one. Not good. If Larry were setting off this morning he'd be blown clear across the lake — that is, if he managed to stay afloat in the six-foot waves that would surely be building up by now.

"What else did Natalie say?" I asked as we tore northward along Highway 8.

"She said that they also had a surprise for us."

"Another surprise? Isn't one enough, with Larry risking his life and Ross's in a boat when he's never even sailed before?"

"Don't be such an alarmist, Michael. You know you always make things out to be worse than they are."

In a field we passed, cows were huddled in a protective circle against the wind.

"With Larry it's impossible to exaggerate. For him even sleeping is a hazardous adventure. You remember Natalie saying that at night Larry's body is blazing hot and soaked with perspiration."

"He's a very intense person."

"Intense? He burns through everything he does. Look at the way he's gone about building a beach cottage."

"He just doesn't want to be extravagant."

"Extravagant? It's true he scoured beach resorts for the cheapest land and bought fourth-grade lumber. But then he designed a cottage that's twice the size of his house before deciding not only to build it himself, but also to wire it so that it blazes with light. And he's got the biggest outhouse I've ever seen. Four seats! You could hold a party in it."

"You must admit that he did look grand up there on the roof of his cottage last fall nailing down those sheets of plywood."

"Grand? I thought he'd kill himself. You'd never get me balancing up there on those two-by-eights."

"No, I wouldn't," Christine agreed.

But I wasn't to be put off. "Any moment, I thought that enormous belly of his — full of pickled herring and salami — would upset his balance and he'd come toppling out of the sky, his body blazing more than ever with all that intensity."

"Well, if that's your attitude, I can see right now you're not going to be pleased with their surprise." Christine's voice had sharpened with disappointment and she tossed her blonde hair back impatiently.

"What has Natalie told you? What else has Larry done? Bought a submarine?" All the while, a voice within me kept whispering, "Careful."

"I promised Natalie I wouldn't tell."

"Wouldn't tell? What is this? A conspiracy?"

"Just a secret, Michael. A secret. Oh, stop sulking."

"I'm not!"

"You should just see yourself in the mirror."

"Okay, but I'm not going to stop until you tell me."

"You're sure you want to know?" Her voice was playful again.

"Oh, come on, Christine, haven't you kept me in suspense long enough?"

"Well, if you must know, he's bought a second beach lot."

"Oh, no! He doesn't suffer enough building one cottage, so he wants to build two?"

"No, that's not it, Michael. He wants *you* to build a cottage. So he's bought *us* a lot. He got it dirt cheap and he thought it would be great if our two families had their vacations together every summer. Natalie said we'll never find a cottage lot any cheaper than $3500. Now maybe you'll stop criticizing him."

"Christine, if I were ever insane enough to start building a cottage out there I'd end up in that cemetery on the road to the lake. Besides, who would want to walk by a cemetery every single time they went sailing?"

"Oh, come on, Michael." Again there was a hint of impatience in her voice. "When did you get so superstitious? Besides, if you ask me, walking by a cemetery sure beats being in one. There's something really attractive about getting off to the lake whenever you want."

"Now you and I both know why Larry has come out to the lake."

"What do you mean?"

"Just to escape his house in the city — it looks like it's been abandoned in the middle of a junkyard."

"It's not that bad."

"It's worse. He's got two cars sitting in his backyard, and you know as well as I do that the only trip those vehicles will ever make again is to the wreckers. He's got three motorcycles — only one of which works. And now this boat. Soon he'll be tinkering with that, too."

"He likes fixing things — unlike some people I know."

"With him, it's more like wrecking things. That house in Winnipeg was brand new when he bought it. But for years now, ever since he decided to build a huge studio in the basement and take the wall out between the living room and dining room, it's been looking as if it's ready for the demolition crew."

"It's true — with the house he has been irresponsible."

So engrossed in the argument had we become that we were missing the cutoff to Arnes. But when I hit the brakes we skidded towards the ditch. Instinctively, I swung the wheel and, at last, the car came round — just — so that now we were heading down the gravel road in the right direction.

I slowed down as we passed the one restaurant in the area. It had a sign out front: *Wir Sprechen Deutsch!*

"Is Larry taking German lessons, do you know?"

"Don't be ridiculous!"

"I guess he didn't realize, when he was looking for Eden, that German was the indigenous language."

"Michael Buchalter, you're outrageous."

"At least we haven't seen anyone tramping around in *lederhosen* yet."

"Look, Michael, let's skip the commentary and get to Larry's cottage."

A few minutes later we stood outside the monumental, unfinished structure. Sunlight glinted on the few windows that had been installed. The walls and floor, built as they were of the cheapest lumber, held invisible tensions within them. None of the boards was straight and they'd had to be wedged and levered into line with the others, and then quickly nailed into place. So although the whole structure looked at rest, in reality it was racked with strains and lines of energy pulling in every direction, all trying to turn and twist, but held in check by the iron will that had nailed it all together. At the door, a second-hand sink waited to be hauled inside. And, leading from the front door to the ground, there was now a single plank that I expected would stay in use till the rest of the cottage was finished, perhaps in the next century.

"Don't say it, Michael," she warned, but I could see that the prospect of Larry walking the plank every day had brought a smile to her lips.

Neither of us said a word when we drove past the cemetery, then turned right and headed toward the beach. As we approached the lake I could see a sail flapping near the shore.

"They haven't gone out on the lake yet." Christine sounded relieved.

But then I took a second glance. Instantly, I brought the car to a halt and at once we were out the doors and racing along the beach. Not thirty-five yards away was the sailboat with Larry and Ross in it. The wind was blowing into a gale, pelting us with sand. Natalie and her younger son, Arthur, were holding on for dear life to the stern of the boat and were being yanked, by savage gusts, step by step into the water.

"Well, you can't complain this time," I heard Natalie call. "There is more than enough wind today for a sail." On the two previous weekends there had been scarcely a breath of air, not even enough to blow out a match.

Holding onto the mainsheet, Ross sat on one side of the boat. Larry stood at the back ready to take command of the tiller. As we came nearer, I could see that the usual blaze about his eyes had, at this point, given way to a look of uncertainty.

"I don't know, Natalie. All this wind. Perhaps . . . "

Natalie, too, must have heard the doubt in his voice, even as she felt the stern slipping from her fingers. "Too late now!" she cried out.

"Don't!" I shouted as the boat sprang forward.

An appalled grimace at once leapt across Larry's face as the boat tore free of Arthur's fingers as well. The look in his eyes as the shoreline quickly receded revealed all: *Lost!* it cried. *We'll never survive a single minute out here!*

I looked further out into the lake. A few seconds more and the boat would be encountering six-foot waves. Now the bow was smashing into one crest after another; white foam was flung against the sail and sprayed into the air. The boat was furiously rocking in those turbulent waters; then it turned and flew along the crest of a wave, starting to plane as it picked up even more speed. All we could see of Larry at this point was his back — immobile, frozen, the tiller locked in his grasp.

"Will they be all right?" Natalie glanced nervously first at me and then at Christine.

"They'll get blown clear across the lake — if they're lucky."

I kept my eyes fixed on Larry, who'd broken out of his trance and now was trying to turn the boat around. Bobbing dangerously on a giant crest, pirouetting first one way and then another, it swung about, started to swamp, and was flung violently into the trough of a wave. At once it broached, and Larry was hurled into the water.

"Oh," cried Natalie, "I should never have let go!"

Ross flung himself backward and seized the tiller. Miraculously, the boat did not capsize, but now it was heading out into the lake again.

"Do something, Michael," Christine shouted.

As I stood there helplessly, a stocky figure came out from one of the lakefront cottages and waved me toward him. I ran forward and saw the canoe lying on the grass in his front yard. It was that or nothing.

"Karl Heinrichs." His hand was outstretched.

"Michael Buchalter." My hand gripped his tightly.

"I have phoned the Coast Guard, but there is no time to wait."

And moments later we were in the water, battling the waves.

"Watch out for that rock." He pointed to a boulder less than a yard away. There was a clipped precision to his words and the trace of a German accent.

We dug our paddles into the water and, by God! I thought, we're actually able to stay afloat — we're even moving forward. The sailboat was still visible, still heading out toward the middle of the lake, but Larry was nowhere in sight. I knew he was a strong swimmer and would be moving towards the shore, but we might pass him if we headed towards the boat. And suddenly there he was being flung past us, riding the waves, his arms and legs moving in a frenzy of motion, burning up the water. At that rate he'd make shore pretty fast. He must have realized Ross was still with the boat and that he could never catch up with it. Now our focus was on the boat again. Sail flapping wildly, mast careening in jerky motions first to one side, then to another, it was steadily moving further into the lake. But then a wild gust spun the boat around on the crest of a giant wave and over it went.

"*Gott sei Dank!*" Karl called out.

Yard by yard we pulled closer, and at last were able to make out Ross clinging to the hull. The canoe rocked wildly in the monstrous waves — almost capsizing — and the spray whistled by our ears. We were still a dangerous twenty-five yards away when Ross caught sight of us and pushed off in our direction. Seconds would pass when, in the roughness of the lake, he was totally lost to us, but then he would appear again like so much flotsam and jetsam hurled about by the fury of wind and waves. And then he was beside us and holding on to the gunwale, his face white as the foam itself, but growing visibly relieved.

"Look!" Karl pointed, and glancing up, I could see two figures in a rescue boat racing toward us. If they kept on as they were, they would soon come upon the sailboat floundering in the water.

Timing our strokes with the waves, we waited for the moment when we could pivot the canoe about and now we were pulling towards the shore.

"Good, Frieda has brought blankets," Karl shouted. And there, sure enough, was Karl's wife by the water's edge, bundling Larry up warmly.

Silently Natalie folded her arms about Ross, and then looked toward Larry. He was staring like a ghost out into the lake. With a blanket wrapped around him, he looked like one of those countless Eastern European refugees in World War II newsreels that recorded the flight of whole populations from invading Nazi armies. Off to one side stood Arthur, a witness to the whole scene, silent, white-faced, clearly puzzled at the way in which his world was being redefined that day.

Then we were able to turn our attention again to the rescue craft, which had located the swamped sailboat. After our own frantic efforts, we were all too aware that those distant, energetic figures certainly knew what they were about.

Beside me, Frieda called out, "They're not the usual crew. Look!"

I took the field glasses from her and gazed out into the lake. At first I could make out only swirling masses of water, but then, at last, I spotted the rubber rescue craft and its crew. They were not stocky and muscular, but tall, blonde and graceful. As one kept control of the rescue craft, the other struggled with the sailboat. Finally she got it on its side, and stood on the keelboard, legs flexed, pumping, arms tugging at the gunwale. And now, haltingly, the mast and sail rose into the air. Quickly she stepped into the boat and soon it was being tugged in the direction of the summer camp opposite them and adjacent to the beach.

The camp was run by an evangelical group whose members we could see, even at this distance, were collecting, choir-like, on the shore. We could hear the chapel bell summoning them to witness the rescue. Snatches of a hymn were caught by the swirling winds:

Jesus loves me
This I know . . .

I glanced at Larry, but he looked as if he had turned into a pillar of salt. What are he and I doing out here in the middle of Goyland? I wondered.

Again, strains from a hymn reached out to us:
O God . . .
Our hope . . .
Our shelter from the stormy blast . . .

"Let's go and pick up the boat," I said. "The chapel bell's ringing, and I think it's tolling for us."

"Oh, shut up!" Christine snapped.

So we all got into the car and drove over to the camp. By the time we had arrived, the rescuers had reached shore amidst tumultous cheers from the assembled company. You'd have thought those two blonde Amazons had come strolling across the water carrying the Holy Ark between them.

"Are you the owner of this boat?" the taller one called.

Larry nodded. It was the most noncommittal nod I'd ever witnessed.

"Were you alone?" asked the other blonde rescuer, who now had a clipboard out and was filling in a form.

"My son." Larry's voice had shrunk to a whisper.

"Pardon."

"I was with my older son."

The taller Amazon looked at him in astonishment. It was only the briefest of glances, but the meaning was clear enough: what kind of a fool would risk his son's life in a lake that had turned into this kind of churning cauldron?

"Any one else with you?" She seemed determined to sound the depths of his folly.

A shake of the head was all Larry could muster.

"No loss of life then. Both captain and crew saved." The information was recorded with a triumphant flourish on one of the forms before her.

"Hallelujah!" cried out the camp director beside us. The crowd of campers pressed still more closely in and picked up the refrain. For a moment I thought they'd break into another hymn, but all that happened was that somebody pulled the chapel bell twice more.

I looked again at our two rescuers — about twenty-two, I would guess, slate-blue eyes, blonde hair bleached almost white by the sun, bodies taut and proud in their achievement, the sort of girls that had haunted our adolescence: long-legged golden girls nurtured by sun and wind, the sort of goddesses that flaunted willing breasts and thighs in our dreams. And actually to meet them at last — and in these circumstances — was the kind of cruel blow that would not be lost on Larry. Why could they not have seen him balanced on the roof of his cottage as he swung sheets of plywood onto the rafters — a titan radiant in the sunlight? A colossus straddling the world. I could imagine Larry returning to his cottage, a slow execution in progress as he walked despondently along the plank to his front door.

When I looked again at Larry, I saw a one-man ghetto.

Somehow, we loaded the boat on top of the car and roped it down. Larry was asked to sign the official forms our rescuers had filled out. We thanked them profusely; we thanked the camp director, nodded to the campers, thanked the wind and sky and sun and water — and turned and fled.

We returned to that stress-ridden cottage — boards pulling and twisting every which way — and sat staring bleakly through window frames that still lacked panes of glass. But unlike the rest of us, Natalie looked as if nothing could ever shake her now. Humming steadily, she busied herself with getting the evening meal, happily aware, once we all sat down, of the unbroken circle around the table.

There was little conversation, but by the time we'd finished dinner — fish with white wine — we'd all calmed down considerably.

"Let's go for a walk," suggested Larry. "It feels good to get away from the city. You see nature in a different way out here."

"So I've noticed."

"Besides, I want to show you something special."

And so we set off on our walk. The wind had died and a light breeze was rustling through the foliage. Perfect weather for an evening sail. But not just yet. The summer had just begun.

Less than eighty feet from his own cottage, Larry pointed out the lot that he had decided was to be ours. Giant trees that would have to be felled, poison ivy to be cleared away, a mammoth structure to be built — straining with unresolved tensions — and finally, to begin and end each day, a plank to be walked.

"Larry, it's a great lot, one of the nicest out here. I'm sure we would never have found it on our own. But thanks, anyway..."

"Thanks anyway? Is that all you can say? Don't you realize we've really gone out on a limb to buy this lot for you? You won't find a better deal on either side of the lake. It's a steal at $3500. I could sell it tomorrow for $4000."

"Oh, good. That's a relief. That's just what you should do. I just don't see us clearing the land and building a cottage. We're city dwellers. Have been for generations."

"Do you agree with this?" Larry asked, turning to Christine.

But after her initial enthusiasm — and her pleasure at having such good friends — I could see that the reality of making the purchase alarmed her.

"I'd have to think more about it," she said.

"What is there to think about? The lot is just five minutes from the lake. You'll never find another bargain like this, not in this lifetime."

Finally our prolonged silence provoked an even more extreme statement: "I want you to know . . . that . . . you're . . . letting us down."

There it was. Out at last: what we'd come rushing out to the lake to hear, after charging into those six-foot waves with the canoe, pulling his son from the drink and then picking up his boat at the camp.

"Let's go to the lake," suggested Natalie, determined to break the impasse. "In the evening you can see right across to the other side."

Christine grew silent as we passed the cemetery and I said not a word. Larry was pointing out all the new cottages that had appeared that summer. "In another year or two they'll have doubled in value."

Further along the shore, we spotted a log of driftwood large enough for us all to sit on and stare out across the water. The lake had calmed down considerably and a swimmer was moving easily out into the distance. He looked as if he could continue with that slow, graceful stroke clear across to the other side. A light flashed from a keelboat making its way further northward. The prospect was inviting. But not that inviting.

I could see that our two families were diverging. But what had taken hold of our separate lives, I couldn't begin to make out. What I did know was that Larry's earlier comment — "I want you to know you've let us down" — still rankled. But perhaps he was justified.

"Look," said Natalie, "there's Karl and Frieda." Slowly they passed before us, a good seventy-five yards out. Their paddles moved slowly, rhythmically together. Then the stroke was interrupted as the wife pointed in our direction. The husband gazed — puzzled for a moment — and then waved his paddle in greeting. Silently we waved back, and a moment later they were again moving through those gently rolling waves.

Still trying to explain, I said, "As a kid, my summers were spent at Winnipeg Beach. Out on the boardwalk and down on the sand, our North End neighbourhood would gather — a whole community. Arnes may be only twenty miles north of there, but it's still a universe away from what I remember. I'd miss all that here."

"And you know what you'd also miss?" Larry snapped. "The french fries with salt and vinegar in a greasy paper bag. Empty pop bottles left on the beach and serviettes blowing along the sand. Our backs and legs peeling because of too much sun. And families squabbling about when they should set off again for the city in the few overcrowded cars."

"You're probably right," I admitted. "I couldn't imagine any of those families coming out here. Not from the North End I knew — with its pedlars and street markets and neighbourhood theatres." That community, I recalled, had been an Old World village where English could often vanish without a trace.

On the lake, about a hundred yards out, the canoeists were crossing back.

"Are they singing?" asked Natalie.

The voices carried faintly across the water, and we strained to catch the words. Then at last we were able to make them out and I found myself abruptly turning away.

"You're influenced too much by things that just don't matter."

Maybe Larry's right, I thought. But I tended to keep an eye out for bad omens — a long family tradition that had gotten my parents and grandparents and uncles and aunts out of Eastern Europe. Everything about this place alarmed me: the cemetery, Larry's cottage writhing in silent agony, and earlier in the day even the lake and sky had screamed their warning. And now these two canoeists paddling among the still-powerful waves rolling toward us. Well, at least they had not been singing *Deutschland Über Alles* as they raced to the rescue this morning.

Yet there was a side of me, I had to admit, that approved of what Larry was doing. It might even be heroic, his battle against ingrained habits, ingrained prejudices, never afraid to appear the fool as he struggled with currents of air and water I would have avoided. I could never have coped with those twisting strains of energy that tore through him as they did through everything he created.

Still, what was the alternative? To draw back into a world that no longer existed? To pull away from the chaos of wind and water, from the cemetery and tolling chapel bell? With German lieder echoing across the lake? Alarming as they all were, something in me admired the foolhardy way Larry faced up to the challenge. Till now I had never thought of myself as being squeamish about such encounters. But it was the violence through which Larry moved that alarmed me. Would he ever learn to accommodate those impulses that had nearly snuffed out two lives this day? Perhaps, back in his studio, he even might be able to harness those turbulent energies, capture them all in his prints. Who knows? I hated to think what fierce creatures might, in time, still manage to peck out his heart and his liver.

When at last we'd said goodbye and set off in the car, it must have been well past midnight. Behind us, in the reddish glow of the tail lights, Larry and Natalie were illuminated for a few moments waving farewell, then vanished into the darkness. At the last, we had been forgiven. Yet all along the side roads, I could feel that empty lot making its claim, tree limbs swaying in the darkness, the wind among the leaves whispering gently. A whole way of life beckoned. Above us the stars sparkled; murmurings from the lake reached out to us. Then turning onto the highway, I felt Christine's head against my shoulder as, exhausted by the day's turbulent events, she fell asleep. In the flowing darkness, the headlights defined only the highway leading southward, while the whole universe strained and twisted with the conflicting forces racing through it. Then, as the car gathered momentum and sprang forward, those two blonde Amazons — those Hallelujah Dream Girls whose breasts and thighs were in no way diminished, but only burnished by time — waved and sang to me from the night sky.

The Ruined Garden

Mr. Samuelson:

That lady down the street, she will yet drive me crazy. Why did I ever buy her house? Sure, it was a good buy in 1987: $140,000. By then that wouldn't have bought you even a garden shed or a run down, secondhand shop or just some old closet space in Toronto, but in Vancouver it was a lot of money to pay, especially for so much trouble. And even if it's worth half as much again now, I'm still not sure it was really worth the price. Since I bought it a year ago, I've been renting the house to that lady who sold it to me, and there's no end of trouble. She blocks the sewer up with tons of rags and kitty litter yet, and then she demands that I unblock it. And locks! She made me put two — some places, three — on every door. And the garden! She never cuts the grass like a tenant is supposed to do. She just lets it run wild. If I could ever get her out, a wrecker I know says he'd bring down that house — locks or no locks — in forty-five minutes flat. By the end of the day, the whole mess would be gone. Carried away in trucks. Not bad for a few thousand dollars.

The Ruined Garden

And four months later, I could have a house standing there worth half a million. Maybe more.

Well, that lady there who sold me the house — her name is Aimée Scott — she is not the easiest person to deal with. Let me tell you what I mean. I was really doing her a favour when I bought that house. She *had* to sell the house — that's what she said. It was mortgaged to the rooftop and she had no money to live on, because that "Bastard of an Ex" wouldn't give her any. That was what she called him: "Bastard of an Ex!" She was lucky she found me. The house was already such a mess I was the only buyer. So just last week she tells me, "My house is now worth $250,000, and all you want to do is wreck it." And when I give her notice, she says she can't move out by December.

"December is my busiest month in the gallery," she says. I should explain she runs an art gallery on Granville Island. Once, I thought, I'll drop by, spend a few dollars on a picture. Maybe even one or two hundred. But those pictures she has there, the cheapest was $600 — for a couple of goldfish swimming through sunlight. And others are two or even three thousand dollars. There is no limit. Even five thousand dollars for an iceberg, I saw. So I went to Zellers and right away I got a few pictures there — a deer, an owl, a train in a valley. No goldfish, but with prices like that I'd settle for sardines in a tin.

You would think a lady with such a fortune in paintings could sell some of them and look after her garden better. Maybe hire somebody to mow the lawn. But no, it's like a jungle in there. Weeds growing three feet high. You could have even tigers prowling around in that grass. Beats me how a lady with such a fine art gallery and pictures worth thousands and thousands of dollars can still have no money. Not even enough money to move.

So she can't move till February, she tells me.

"I'm sorry," I say, "but the wrecker has only time in December. And we agreed, you remember, that I only had to give you two months' notice."

"Yes, but nobody moves in December. It's just too inconvenient in December, Mr. Samuelson. That's when I do the bulk of my year's business."

"I'm sorry. I didn't realize that by you December was such a busy month."

So I speak to the wrecker, Oscar Kopinski. "What about February?"

"In February, already I have twenty houses coming down. In the West End mainly. It will look like Stalingrad there before I'm through. But you tell her — tell her! — it has to be December. Who owns that house anyway, Lew?"

"But she will have lawyers. She could sue me. She is already suing her Ex for everything he's got. Maybe that's why she has no money now, but by tomorrow she could be a wealthy lady again."

"So? It's not your house? Who's to say no if you want to tear it down in December?"

"Let it be February, Oscar. So you'll tear down twenty-one houses that month."

Oscar shrugged, "February then."

So what does she do? She sends me notice she's moving the end of September. But by then I have no wrecker. What am I to do?

I go right away to her place. Then I notice not only the grass and weeds and flowers growing like a jungle, but now everywhere there are cats. I knew she had a few house cats, but cats on the steps? Cats on the carport roof at the back? Cats in the windows? Then from the corner of my eye I see a German shepherd across the street. At first, he looks like he will leap across the road and swallow whole three kittens playing there on the sidewalk. Then he sees all those cats: there are cats on the sidewalk; cats in that jungle of flowers by the steps; in the grass there are cats that, sure enough, look like miniature tigers — a whole world of cats, a house alive with cats inside and out. And the German shepherd ducks his head low in the grass and begins to back away. Turns around, takes a look behind and then *runs* into the lane. *Fast!*

I walk up the stairs and there are eyes everywhere staring at me. I try the doorbell, but nothing happens. So I knock on the door. Once. Twice. The eighth time she answers.

When I come into the living room cats scurry off in all directions. She must have twenty or thirty cats there now. When all is still, I look again at Mrs. Scott. I'd forgotten how short she is. A plump little lady, in a dark suit, with a tie yet, black shiny hair — not a curl out of place, like she just had it done at the beauty parlor — and glasses with a sparkling blue frame.

"Look, Mrs. Scott. We agreed. You wanted to leave in February."

"I can't afford to wait till then. I need the money to rent a less expensive place."

"What is this 'can't afford'? You have the money from the house. You have an art gallery. And all those paintings. Thousands and thousands of dollars, they cost."

"They're all on consignment. I haven't sold a painting in weeks. And, in the meantime, the lawyers have gobbled up my bank account. It's expensive suing people, Mr. Samuelson."

"But I need the money."

"So do I."

"What will I tell the wrecker? He's busy now. It was all arranged — for February. You said so yourself."

"Tell him if he doesn't come when you want him, then you'll sue him."

So angry I was when I looked at her that I didn't know what to do. Such a small, plump lady. Yet like steel she is. I could see now why no husband would stay with her. Three times she was divorced, I heard from her neighbour Henry. Anyone can see he likes her. He's sixty-five, if he's a day, yet he wants to have again a girlfriend. On Sundays she has lunch with him. And he wears such fancy suits, you wouldn't believe.

Before today, I thought he is crazy. She will never marry a man more than fifteen years older than herself. Now — I don't know. If she has no money and nowhere else to go, maybe . . . Yet in the house there are such fancy things — a dishwasher, three telephone-answering machines on three separate lines, fancy cameras and, in the living room, what is it called? A harps-his-chord. And all those cats. A fortune she must spend just to feed them all.

"These cats — what will happen to them when you move?"

"Oh," her voice got all soft, "do you want some? There's a cute kitten, part Siamese, you could have. And a fluffy black one with a white face. His name's Warlock. But this tortoiseshell cat I'm keeping."

I could see that they'd all come out — from under the couch, the easy chair, by the doorways of the kitchen and bedroom — and were looking at me.

"No, no, my wife and me — we have no time for cats. But where will you take them? Not into an apartment. It isn't allowed."

"It's all that bastard's fault. Max gave my son Jeremy a kitten for his fourteenth birthday. She was just a little ball of fluff. We had gotten down to only one cat — this tortoiseshell one — and she was too old to have any more kittens. But look at us now just three years later."

And I could see what she meant: cats, cats, everywhere. "Your husband from before, he's a joker maybe?"

"He's a bastard. I'd blow him up if I could. Do you know what it costs to feed twenty-four cats every month?"

"So they eat you out of house and home and now you have to move?"

"Oh, I would have had to move anyway."

"And your husband from before? He doesn't help you?"

"My Ex? He won't even pay for Jeremy to go to university next year."

"He is a painter, I know. I saw in your gallery windows his paintings. But you haven't sold them. Maybe he has no money."

"Money? He's got money alright. He just moved into a big, new house in Point Gray with that bitch he married six years ago. But, dammit, she still looks hardly old enough to hold a driver's licence. And he's given her a shiny new Porsche to zip around town in. While I have to make do with that rusty old tin can of a Toyota."

"He is a successful painter then, your husband from before?"

"His paintings are in the best galleries."

"And even by you, in your small gallery."

"Of course he's in my gallery. At least, he was in my gallery until a few days ago, when all of his paintings and prints were stolen."

"Stolen? *Oi, veh!* You must be upset. And your husband from before, he must be upset too."

"That bastard?"

"You don't feel sorry for him?"

"Sorry? I hate him. Can't you understand? How many times do I have to tell you? It's his work I like."

"And me? Do you like my work too? Will you move in February like we agreed? Mrs. Scott, if you move now, the place will stand empty. I'll lose $4,000."

"I've already told you I can't afford to stay."

"But these cats you can afford to keep. These paintings, this harps-his-chord, this furniture."

"Mr. Samuelson, I told you I'm leaving at the end of September. Provided I can find an apartment."

"So you might stay then?"

"Goodbye, Mr. Samuelson."

She was like a duchess, the way she spoke. I could see why her husbands left. Like steel, she is. Poor Henry. He doesn't know what he's starting up with: one lady, twenty-four cats, at least, three husbands from before, a son, a harps-his-chord and paintings upon paintings — mostly of goldfish and icebergs.

While I was walking down the steps, I could feel all those eyes — dozens of eyes at the windows and in the tall weeds and grass — staring at me. Did her husbands from before feel the same way with who knows how many eyes staring at them as they walked away for the last time?

So now I'll have to talk to Oscar Kopinski. I just hope she doesn't change her mind again.

Max the Bastard:

"Hi. This is Max. Neither Vicky nor I can come to the phone right now, but if you'll leave a message after the beep, one of us will get back to you as soon as possible."

"Hello, Max, you bastard. This is the third time today I've tried to get you, but all I get is this damn machine. Look, I've just spoken with the owner of what used to be our house and I have to move in ten days. And I have no place to go and no money to go with. Now stop behaving like such a little creep and phone me back. At once, do you hear?"

"Oh, yeah, fat chance she has of my phoning her back. 'Max, you bastard' — why does she always call me that, Vicky?"

"I guess because she's hurting and she sees you as the cause of her pain. Is she often that angry?"

"Only when she knows she won't get her way. And lately that's become more and more often."

"Do I ever sound like that?"

"Only when you don't get *your* way."

"And how often is that?"

"Not bloody often."

"But why is she *so* angry?"

"Well, she does have to move soon. It must be a shock leaving that house after twenty years."

"I guess she was hoping some day you might come back — as long as there was a place to come back to."

"One look at you, Vicky, would have convinced her otherwise."

"But she's never met me."

"You can be sure, though, that sometime during these last six years she's seen you."

"So she gets angry and phones."

"Won't do much good. Only reminds me of what I've left."

"But she does need the money, Max."

"She always needs money."

"For the move and for an apartment."

"And for the three phone lines and the two parking spots on Granville Island, and for all those lawyers she's hired to sue me. She doesn't do anything by half measures. She's an extravagant lady, my ex-wife."

"Well, you must admit, Max, that was an extraordinary thing to do — running into her art gallery the other day, when only her helper was there, and stealing all your prints and paintings."

"But they were *mine*."

"Max, they were part of the divorce settlement. They were *hers*."

"I didn't know they would become so valuable in just six years. Besides, she hadn't paid me a penny for those other paintings of mine — the ones she'd sold on consignment. Those paintings *really* were mine."

"Your paintings and prints are the only ones she's ever earned any real money on at that gallery."

"Why are you suddenly so defensive of her? Are you two pals now? You meet and have coffee behind my back?"

"I just don't like to be hated by someone I don't even know. And if she doesn't have any money for food and rent . . ."

"And for those cats. Don't forget the cats."

"Well, you know, Max, who's responsible for those . . ."

"How was I to know that one kitten would trigger a population explosion? Anyway, she could have had it spayed."

"If she'd had any money."

"Jeremy liked that kitten. Remember how happy he was on his birthday when I got it for him?"

"Oh, come on, Max, no one gives a fourteen-year-old a tiny kitten. You knew that kitten was a booby trap. He only took it so as not to hurt your feelings."

"Well, she's done some pretty catty things to me, too."

"Like what?"

"Like that harpsichord."

"I must admit that harpsichord was a bit much."

"I just wanted to get her a gift — to celebrate our reconciliation."

"But, Max, you were still seeing me then, remember? Some reconciliation!"

"She didn't know that."

"Oh, Max, why else do you think she asked for that particular harpsichord?"

"Like a fool, I even made out the cheque to Marty myself. Aimée must have thought that was pretty funny — my helping out her ex-boyfriend when he was short of cash."

"Were you really that surprised, Max? Why shouldn't she acquire a boyfriend while you and I were off in Mexico?"

"A man's kind of fragile that way, Vicky."

"Well, maybe she's kind of fragile, too. You never told me that you had a eleven-year-old son. I still can't believe I went off to Mexico with you a few weeks after we met."

"It wasn't as if I was hiding anything. I just didn't think of mentioning it."

"It wasn't that important, Max?"

"Of course it was important. But I didn't realize that we'd be getting so involved with one another."

"Aimée did, though. That's why she gave up Marty."

"Well, it sure didn't take him long to find someone else — someone who wouldn't present him with an instant family."

"Still, it was *you* she wanted, Max."

"But she kept phoning Marty. Why, I even heard she offered to come over one night and make that relationship a threesome."

"Only because you were still seeing me, Max."

"That little bitch!"

"Poor love. And when did you start feeling so angry?"

"When she started to play that damn harpsichord every evening as soon as I got back from the studio."

"And why do you suppose she did that?"

"Okay, okay, so what if you *were* at the studio, too? An artist needs the right ambience, you know."

"I must admit that harpsichord does puzzle me. Why would she keep it — and play it — if she was so determined to win you back?"

"Because she's dumb, that's why. She's dumb."

"Have you ever considered, Max, that the harpsichord was her insurance policy?"

"Some insurance policy. You know what that harpsichord insured? It insured I'd never come back."

"Exactly. Maybe that's just what she intended."

"Intended?"

"That you never come back — no matter how much she might waver."

"She got me to pay so that she would be insured from my ever coming back? Is that what you're saying?"

"Oh, you are clever! You see, you finally have figured it out."

"Well, I hope she likes playing it out on the street, because once that house gets torn down, that's where she's going to have to play it. All by herself. Or maybe all those cats can join in with a chorus or two."

"Have you ever wondered, Max, if Aimée could be right?"

"Right? How do you mean?"

"Maybe you are a bastard."

"Oh, God, don't *you* start in now."

Christine:

"Yes, operator. Yes, I'll accept the charges."

"Hello, Chris. Thank God you're at home."

"Aimée, how have you been?"

"Terrible!"

"What's the matter?"

"It's that bastard Max."

"Look, Aimée, if you're going to complain about my ex-brother-in-law again, maybe I should phone you tonight — on the Nite Owl Rate after eleven."

"How can you think of pinching pennies at a time like this? My house is about to come tumbling down around my ears and you think of pinching pennies."

"Aimée, I just can't afford any more hour-long conversations at these rates. That last bill almost resulted in divorce proceedings around here. Do you realize you were ranting on about Max for nearly *two* hours?"

"This won't take long. I'm phoning from the gallery and a customer may come in at any moment."

"I'm glad to hear business is picking up."

"It's terrible. Haven't sold a painting in weeks. The last people to come in were two middle-aged women who asked if I'd call them a taxi."

"Did they buy anything?"

"They didn't even give me a quarter for the phone."

"I guess October's a slow month in the art world."

"Every month's slow — until December."

"Well, that's something to look forward to."

"But before then Jeremy and I have to find an apartment. And I need money for the movers and for the rent and for a damage deposit . . . Christine, are you still there?"

"Look, Aimée, we're still paying last month's telephone bill."

"Aren't they terrible? But the government is putting pressure on the phone companies to smarten up. Whoops! Hold on a minute . . . There. All's well again."

"What was that all about?"

"I brought Lucy and Mable to the gallery this morning because they're both in heat and I had to get them away from Big Sam. But some damn tomcat was trying to climb through the window and I had to shut it. Then I thought I saw Max down at the end of the street. I'll bet *he* had a hand in this."

"You mean to tell me you still haven't had those cats spayed? I sent you close to two hundred dollars for that vet on Oak Street."

"I just haven't had the time, Chris."

"But I thought business was slow these last few weeks."

"That's no reason to kill it off altogether by closing the gallery. Once word gets around that you're unable to continue, you're finished. Don't you know even that much? I'll have all my artists wanting to place their work with another dealer."

"How many cats do you have now, Aimée?"

"I haven't counted lately."

"More than ten?"

"Probably."

"More than fifteen?"

"For God's sake, Chris, I can't take the time right now to conduct a cat census."

"Not more than twenty? Oh, Aimée, not more than twenty! If this keeps up you'll be known as the Cat Lady of Vancouver."

"Look, Chris, I would never have expected my own sister and brother-in-law to become so . . . so middle class . . . You're totally brainwashed to worry about nickels and dimes and what the neighbours will think.

"Yes, I really am disappointed, Chris, at how conditioned you've become by all of Michael's views. Worrying about cats and long-distance charges. Beneath all that easygoing, liberal manner of his, I suspect there's a dyed-in-the-wool chauvinist."

"You can't even afford to feed all those cats."

"They're small. They don't eat all that much. Besides, they're cute."

"It's *incestuous*, Aimée. What you've got there is some primitive kingdom that's rampant with inbreeding and incest. They probably don't even look like ordinary cats anymore."

"Now that you mention it, some of them do look kind of stunted and . . . "

"And . . . ?"

"Well, some of them do have crooked tails or very short tails or almost no tails at all."

"Oh, those poor little kittens. What does Jeremy say about this?"

"He doesn't mind, as long as none of them come down into the basement to his room."

"Why is your son living in the basement?"

"Why not?"

"Why not? Now look, Aimée, don't get uppity with me — especially *not* on long distance that I'm paying for. My God! Long distance!"

"See — just what I suspected — you've been brainwashed by Michael."

"Don't complain to me about Michael or I'll hang up. But before I do at least give me the satisfaction of an answer. Why is your teenage son sleeping in the basement?"

"Because the cats live on the main floor."

"So Jeremy sleeps in the basement?"

"He likes it there. He likes the privacy."

"Oh, Aimée, what will become of you both?"

"If you'll stop prattling on and on about the cats, I'll tell you. The house is being demolished on the first of October. I need to move in ten days, and I was wondering if you'd like to buy one of Max's paintings. I'll even knock 25% off the asking price."

"How much?"

"It's worth four thousand dollars. You can have it for three."

"You're kidding."

"Chrissy, stop behaving like a philistine."

"We don't need a painting. Especially not of icebergs. It's cold enough in Winnipeg."

"But you do."

"What for?"

"To protect you against Michael's middle-class prejudices. It'll be your . . . *insurance* policy!"

"But will it protect me against his screams, Aimée, when he sees the bill for this telephone call?"

"You bet it will."

"Aimée, I'll start screaming soon myself. I need one of Max's paintings about as much . . . as much as you need that damn harpsichord."

"That harpsichord gives me a great deal of pleasure, I'll have you know."

"I'm sure it gave Max a great deal of pleasure as well, especially when you told him it was Marty's."

"In the evenings I can play for hours, and I forget all about moving and bills and the gallery and that bastard Max."

"Oh, Aimée."

"It's pleasant, Chrissy. And all the cats and kittens stop racing from room to room and across the counters and windowsills. They all become silent and some of them even cuddle up around me."

"Aimée, stop it! That's enough! I'll send you the $3000."

"And I'll get Max's painting off to you right away."

"I can hardly wait."

"But you must insure it. In case it gets stolen. Insure it for $4000. And whatever you do, don't store it in the basement. The damp will ruin the canvas."

"Can we hang up now, Aimée? Please? Before I remember how much I hate Max's paintings? Especially the ones of icebergs."

"Sure, Chrissy, sure. I didn't really mean to suggest you were brainwashed . . . "

"Oh, I know that."

"And that Michael was an arrogant snob, though . . . "

"Though . . . ?"

"Though I do believe, if you really thought about it, you'd see that he and Max are not totally . . . "

"Look, Aimée, I have to get off this phone."

"Of course, Chrissy. I understand. Your sister who's being evicted phones to ask for help, and all you can think of is not antagonizing that middle-class, chauvinist husband of yours with a long-distance telephone bill."

"I'm hanging up, Aimée."

"Just one last thing, Chrissy."

"Make it short."

"Now don't get mad?"

"Who's mad? I may be crazy, but I'm not mad. Not yet."

"Well, listen, do you think you could courier me the money? I'm really desperate."

"Why not? It's just money. Just our savings. Just my marriage that's at stake here, that's all."

"And if you could get that cheque certified, that would be miraculous. Just miraculous. And couriering it would only cost another twelve dollars."

"And what's twelve dollars when you already owe so much?"

"Exactly."

"And besides, Aimée, I'll bet the cats are out of kitty litter."

"Never mind, I'll pay you back every penny I owe you once I get back on my feet again. Tell you what: I'll even sell your painting for you once I have time to find a buyer. In fact, you may as well leave 'Blue Iceberg' here with me — save crating and shipping charges — and I'll put your name on it."

"Sure."

"And one more thing."

"What?"

"Don't sound so suspicious."

"Who's suspicious? Why should I sound suspicious? I have no need to sound suspicious, have I?"

"Since I'm going to have to leave here in ten days, you can reach me after that at Henry's next door. You want the phone number and address?"

"I already have it."

"From before?"

"When you walked out on Max the first time."

"Yes, you can reach me at Henry's."

"Wait a minute, Aimée. You're not moving permanently into Henry's, are you?"

"Yes, initially . . . "

"I thought you were moving into an apartment."

"I am, but not before the Christmas sales are over. You know that's my busy season. I only have time now to move next door."

"Does Henry know you're moving in?"

"He won't mind."

"You mean you haven't asked him?"

"Look, Chris, I'm pretty busy right now. I really have to hang up — someone has just walked into the gallery. Talk to you again when I'm more settled. And don't forget to courier that cheque to me right away. Thanks a million."

Jeremy:

I don't know what Mom got so upset for. Or Dad either. I was only trying to help. Mom had been working herself up into a frenzy about having to pack up the house before it all got pulled down at the end of the month. So I thought, if I couldn't get my own apartment, I'd store all my stuff at Dad's place. But when I pulled up in that van I'd rented, you'd have thought I was a stranger asking for a handout. You could see it in his face when he answered the door.

"So what's up?"

"Just thought I'd drop over to say 'Hi'."

"So why that huge van? Hey, you ran over the flowerbed on the right-hand side of the driveway."

"Sorry about that, Dad."

At first, I wasn't even sure if he was going to invite me in, but then Vicky came to the door and gave me a big hug. "Long time no see, stranger. How about some coffee?"

That seemed to wake Dad up, and now he was the way I could still remember him. As we walked into the living room he put his arm across my shoulders, sort of affectionately, like half a hug — or maybe it was just to steer me past the bric-a-brac. Mom says I'm at an awkward age, but that's no reason for Dad to keep me out of his house. You see, everything in that house of his is white — everything! White rugs, white sofa and chair, white drapes. You'd think you were in the Arctic and needed sunglasses to protect your eyes from the glare. There's just the odd touch of pale blue here and there, in the light fixtures and window trimmings. It's a bit like living in one of his paintings — all peaceful and quiet, but pretty cold, too. At any rate, that's the phase he's in now.

"Jeremy, just what is that you're tracking onto the carpet?"

"The carpet?"

"Yes, what is that brown stuff on the carpet?"

"Max, I think it's . . . "

"Is this some sort of a joke, Jeremy? Has your mother . . . ?"

"Gosh, Dad, I'm sorry. But with all those cats, it's always a hazard. I must have stepped in it when I was loading up the van. I should have realized by the smell that was following me over here. Have you got some Javex or Ajax or something? I'll clean it up right away."

Dad was starting to look pretty mad. It's easy to recognize that 'you're-interfering-with-my-life-again look', but Vicky, as usual, came to my rescue.

"It's all right, Jeremy. I'll look after it. Just take off your shoes and put them outside."

In ten minutes she had everything right as rain again. And that frozen look on Dad's face was beginning to melt away.

"So what have you got in the van, Jeremy?"

"All my things. We have to move out of the house next week. It's getting torn down."

"I know. Found a new place yet?"

"Mom's been looking."

"And you?"

"Well, I've been looking, too."

"Where?"

"That's what I wanted to talk to you about. There's an apartment just a few blocks away from here — right near the water."

"Around here?"

"It's a neat place, Dad. You'd really like it."

"But we're right near Jericho Beach here. Apartments must be going at $1500 a month. At least."

"This one's $2000. Really nice, Dad. With a place like that, I just know I could do really well at school. Jogging along beside the water every morning. Great view of the mountains while I'm doing my homework."

"You're kidding."

"It's just too good to be true, Dad. A real find. The apartment is empty right now and I could even move in today. But they want a damage deposit as well as the first month's rent. So what do you say?"

Dad's coffee seemed to have gone down the wrong way. He started coughing, then choking. His face got all red, redder than I've ever seen it. Even redder than when he and Mom are fighting. Vicky got all upset, too, and started patting him on the back, lightly at first. But then she really had to wallop him a few times before he could finally catch his breath. She hit him so hard his top plate flew out onto the carpet.

"I really don't think so, Jeremy," he finally managed to gasp.

"But it's a neat apartment, Dad. All my friends think it's just great. And you've been saying I should move out — away from Mom — and become independent. You said so yourself."

"Part of being independent, Jeremy, is paying your own way."

"But you did say, Dad, you'd help me out. At first, anyway. Remember?"

"Jeremy, this is impossible. Your independence is just going to have to wait a bit longer."

"But, Dad, this apartment is a rare find. Apartments like this one don't come along every day. And it's got more than enough room to store all my things."

"Your things?"

"What I've got in the van."

"What is in that van, Jeremy?"

"Oh, you know, Dad. My three uniforms for cadets. And the military helmets and boots. And my other uniforms too. You know, the ones Mom helped me find in all those antique shops on Granville Island: uniforms from World Wars I and II, and sabres and gas masks and battle flags and spurs and officers' belts and coats."

"So you need a whole van for those?"

"There's also some of the presents from my birthdays: my model airplanes and trucks and cowboy outfits. I know it's kind of silly keeping all that stuff, Dad, but it doesn't seem right just to dump it all. And there's that Children's Encyclopedia you got me and the chemistry set and telescope and the Monopoly game and Chinese checkers and chess books. I mean it's my whole childhood, really — a kind of giant security blanket that's kept me together when everything else was falling apart."

"You can't be serious."

"And then there's all my clothing — my fifteen jackets, twenty-two pairs of trousers, eight suits and two hundred ties. Most of it is like new, Dad. You don't expect me to give away all my clothes, do you? Some of those things I hardly wore."

"Jeremy, you've outgrown most of those things — except for the ties."

"But like I said . . . they're like new, Dad. Don't you understand? You want me to throw all those things — everything — away? Into the garbage can?"

"Now, Jeremy, stop being so melodramatic. They won't get dumped into the garbage. I'm sure the Salvation Army will be more than happy . . . "

"You mean I can't store them here? There just isn't any place else. And you've already said you won't help me rent that apartment."

"But, Jeremy, you know you'll never — not in a million years — use any of that stuff again. You know that."

"But they're *mine*, Dad."

Then he was silent for a while, and I thought for sure now he'll give in.

"I'm sorry, Jeremy. There's just no room here. I know you think two storeys and ten rooms is a lot of space, but it's all taken. I mean the studio and the study take up the better part of a whole floor. And all the other rooms — well, they're full, too . . . full of . . . full of . . . "

"Yeah, Dad, I know, full of . . . ambience."

Vicky got all red in the face, then, and ran out of the room.

Not a bad idea, I thought, and got up to leave.

"No need to get mad, Jeremy. Look, why don't you stay for dinner?"

Now I really was mad and wished I still had on my cat-shit shoes to tramp all over Dad's white carpet again.

"Did your mother put you up to this, Jeremy? Has she . . . ?"

But I was already out the front door and down the front stairs. The van started up with a roar, and as I backed out — over those same flowerbeds — I saw Dad's face cringing in pain.

That made me madder still, but when I looked up to check in the mirror for traffic, I could see those same features in my own face — and that same pain — reflected back at me. So by the time I got to the end of the block, I was beginning to suspect that the look on Dad's face really had little to do with the flowerbeds.

When I got back home — and Mom learned where I'd been — right away she started to rant on about Dad the way she does. But I wouldn't let her get away with a thing.

"Why?" she finally asked in exasperation, "why must you always defend him?"

Henry:

Well, today has been quite the day — a noisy day. I almost fell out of bed this morning when Aimée phoned.

"Hi, Henry. It's me."

"Who's me?"

"Marilyn Monroe."

"Well, Marilyn, Henry isn't in right now, but will I do?"

"Who are you?"

"Clark Gable."

"Sorry, Clark Gable, but my heart belongs to Henry."

"Oh, shucks, now. But if you're sure, I'll tell Henry."

"You tell him I'm coming over right away. I've something important to ask him."

And less than a minute later, I heard her come skipping up the stairs. Now, Aimée's not the lightest creature in the world, but she actually came *skipping* up those steps.

"But, Aimée, we'll be the scandal of the neighbourhood."

"It's about time this neighbourhood had a scandal."

"But where will you put all your things?"

I could see that did stop her for a moment. I should explain that the house — and the backyard — are filled with things I've collected over a lifetime. Street signs, pickaxes, six antique cars, a couch, chairs, aluminum siding, electric wiring, five cans of tar, eight bicycles, a birdhouse, sinks, two wagons, pots, pans, a washing machine, dryer, dishes — not to mention a thirty-year subscription to the *Vancouver Sun*. Haven't missed an issue, either. In fact, it was when the newspapers reached

The Ruined Garden

the ceiling in every room of the house that Julia left me fifteen years ago.

"It's either me or all that junk," she insisted one Friday night when I came home from work at the insurance company. "Now I don't want to be unreasonable, Henry. It doesn't all have to go at once. We could . . . we could hold garage sales, and after a few months whatever we couldn't sell, we'd get carted off to the junkyard."

But even as she spoke the words, she must have known I'd never give in. "Henry, please. It's just junk." And she looked for a long while into my eyes.

"I'm not going to give it up."

After she left, there was a bit of extra space, but that filled up pretty soon.

"Well listen, Aimée, there has to be a clear understanding between you and me."

"An understanding?"

"About what stays and what goes."

"I couldn't agree more, Henry."

"All my stuff stays. Everything."

"That's okay with me."

"It is?"

"So long as none of my things get thrown out."

"Like?"

"Like Jeremy's military uniforms, the aquarium, the desks, filing cabinets and — oh, yes — the harpsichord."

"The harpsichord?"

"You bet. There must be space in one of the rooms."

I paused for a moment, stared out from the hallway into the living room, packed to the ceiling with plumbing fixtures, car batteries, transmission gears, trunks, tables, chairs, and old newspapers, then started to shake my head.

"Let's get one thing straight, Henry. If the harpsichord can't stay, neither can I."

"Well, I suppose I could move the spare bathtub out of the livingroom . . . and a few of the electric motors. I could just cover them with a tarpaulin in the yard — in the space where I usually park the car. I'll leave the Chevette on the street."

"It's a deal — so long as there's room for my stuff somewhere."

"It can all stay. I just have to figure out where to put it. How long will you be moving in for?"

"I might as well tell you, Henry, I couldn't find an apartment — at least not for the money I can afford."

"So how long, Aimée? How long?"

"For the duration, Henry. Just like you've been asking me to all these years."

"When?"

"Tomorrow morning. It'll take me at least that long to finish packing up all my boxes and round up all the cats."

"The cats?"

"Of course, the cats."

"I hadn't thought about the cats."

"And all my plants."

"Plants?"

"The geraniums, roses, mums, violets, zinnias, snapdragons, peonies. Plants, Henry, plants!"

"But where will we put them all?"

"We'll make room, Henry. Lots of room. Don't be such a fuss-budget."

"But the house will become . . . so cluttered."

"You won't even notice *us*, Henry."

"Us?"

"Jeremy and me."

"Oh, yes, I'd forgotten about Jeremy."

So I sort of nodded and gave her a key to the front door and went off for a walk. I had to think. How would we all manage? I went into the back lane and looked into her backyard. Wild roses and peonies growing everywhere in the grass that was almost as tall as a person in places. Jays and wild canaries flew in among the bushes and trees. And at the back, on the roof of the carport, a colony of cats lolled about in the sunlight.

Frankly, when I got back to the house, I was tempted to call the whole deal off, but I thought, it can wait till tomorrow. Let her get some rest. Maybe in the morning I'll feel differently about it. Right now her moving in just didn't make sense — even to me. I used to ask her regularly every week, but after a few years I guess I thought she'd never take me up on it. Then as I was falling asleep that night, the solution suddenly came to me. I could store a lot of her stuff in the six old cars in the driveway. Maybe I could store Jeremy there, too.

Oscar the Wrecker:

From what Lew Samuelson had told me, I kind of expected, when I pulled up in front of Mrs. Scott's house at the end of September, that anything might happen. And sure enough, she was standing by the main entrance, looking as if she was ready to throw herself in front of the backhoe or front-end loader to stop me from tearing down her house. I had warned my crew that there might be trouble. And, to make matters worse, she was with a whole gang of her friends, just waiting for us. But then I realized they were there to help her carry boxes into the house next door, and had just stopped for a moment to watch us pull in. When she caught sight of me, she marched right over and asked, "How long do you think it'll take?"

"To bring it down?"

"Yes. And to cart it away."

"To bring it down will take about an hour — maybe a bit less, maybe a bit more. To cart it all away and tidy up a little — well, you can never tell for sure. But by the end of the day, we'll all be gone."

"Along with my house!"

"Now, don't blame me, lady. This is all between you and Lew Samuelson. He told me you wanted now and not February."

"No, no, I'm not mad at either of you. It's my Ex I have to thank for this."

"Well, that's his lookout then."

"That's for sure."

And when I looked into her face, I thought, watch out, buddy, whoever you are. This lady will not stop till she's sliced you up thinner than the meat in a pastrami sandwich.

"Do you mind if I take some photos? I want to capture the whole operation from beginning to end."

Well, that sure beat me. A real new one, that was. "Sure, snap whatever you want. Just watch out for the falling boards and stucco. Here, I'll lend you a hard hat. We should be ready to start in about an hour."

It took about that long to station the backhoe and go through the house to salvage anything that we could sell later. And we did not bad: an oak fireplace mantle, a bevelled mirror, a pair of French doors, even a spiral staircase twelve feet high. We were lucky. For a change, we'd gotten into the house before the scavengers did. They'll usually break in the night before a house comes down — even if they have to cut a hole in a sidewall because the doors have been bolted shut and the windows boarded up. They don't expect to find anyone home at that point. But I could see that Mrs. Scott would have scared anybody off, just with her camera.

And so an hour later, when we started, there she was in a hard hat — that short, plump, little lady — with a glint in her eyes and a fancy camera in her hands. I tell you, taking down that house was different from any other job I've done — and believe me, I've done some lulus: a warehouse on the wharf, once, where the backhoe almost toppled into the water; an office building constructed like a bomb shelter — to last forever; a bank with a huge vault, steel door and everything, and even a parking lot with cement ramps. You'd have to be a five-star general to manoeuvre around some of these jobs. But this was different. I've done lots of houses — they're easy. This one, though, was like a play, a performance. We would wait till she was set and then I brought the backhoe up to the house, lifted the boom, and — whoosh — the bucket passed through the roof, the ceilings, the front wall and, bite by bite, right down through the floor of the house to the basement. Then up went the boom again, and with two more passes the bucket was taking down the sidewall, chimney and everything. All the time, that camera of hers was clicking away, catching everything: the shingles scattering and bricks flying, windows shattering and walls buckling. It was as if we were actors in a movie, celebrities, and we would all find our pictures in the papers the next day.

Then we brought the backhoe around through the yard — the carport didn't take us five minutes — and started in on the house from behind. Soon the engine of the backhoe was roaring louder than ever, and then, finally, the house gave a wrench on its foundation and split apart. All of a sudden — it was gone. But Mrs. Scott was ready for that, too. She kept darting in everywhere. We had to be careful that the bucket didn't grab *her*. Trees a foot or two feet thick got torn out of the ground, along with row upon row of shrubbery that looked so nice and rich I wouldn't have minded having some of it at my place. And there she was snapping picture after picture as the trees got swung away and cut into pieces with a chain saw.

Believe me, it's no small operation tearing down a house. Waterpipes, sinks, light fixtures, kitchen cabinets, doors torn off their hinges — she was determined that nothing in that house should be forgotten. Every board, every brick, every shingle had its picture taken. What is she planning? To make a photograph album so that when she is old she will show it to her grandchildren?

When she stopped to load her third roll into the camera, I came over to where she was standing beside the mountain of junk that had once been her house. "Mrs. Scott — these photos you're taking — when they're developed, could you make me some copies?"

"If you like. But why?" I could see she was surprised.

"I thought it would be nice to have. To show people — customers — all that I have to do. To them $3500 for knocking down a house seems a lot. They should see it's no small job."

"And is that the only reason?"

I hadn't expected such a question, but finally I said, "I would like to have something — later, when I'm too old to work — something to look at. To remind me of what I used to do every day."

"But what for? I don't understand."

"What's not to understand? Mr. Samuelson, he tells me you have an art gallery. People want pictures to look at. They pay thousands of dollars, he tells me. For what? For minnows swimming in sunlight? Or for some icebergs that just sit there and won't even melt?"

"I'll send you copies of everything."

"But tell me, Mrs. Scott. What for are you taking all these pictures? For some kind of album, maybe?"

"Yes. And I'm going to send it to my Ex — the bastard who ran out on Jeremy and me."

"But why? They will give him only pleasure."

"Oh, no, they won't. Take my word for it. He won't find any pleasure in these."

Then I saw that the men were waiting, so I got back to the job. Now we began loading everything into the dump trucks: beams, stucco, floorboards, plaster, two-by-fours, windows, pipes. There's a lot to a house and the trucks kept coming and going all afternoon.

But finally it was all done and the backhoe and front-end loader and the trucks and the men were all gone. There was just me standing beside my car. Then I saw Mrs. Scott waving from the front window of the house next door, and I waved back.

But why? I asked myself, as I got into the car. Why would she send all those photos to that bastard of an Ex? It doesn't make sense. To let him see what he has done? For such a man, it is a waste of time.

And then as I drove off, I understood. Yes, she is a very determined lady, that Mrs. Scott — just like Lew Samuelson said. With those photos, her Ex will see — she will show him — just what she is going to do to his life. Maybe he might not understand right away, but over the years — and after all the lawsuits — he will finally figure it out.

That Mrs. Scott, she sure is some lady — racing in and out between the machines, jumping out of the way of the falling stucco and two-by-fours — taking photo after photo. At first, when I saw her standing there in front of her house, I didn't know what to expect. But it didn't take long before I really got to like her. And now I know why. With all her business contacts, and with all those pictures for advertising, we could go into business together, the both of us. Yes, we could be partners — maybe even in more ways than one!

Henry:

That night, after all the men and machinery had left, Aimée and I stood by the side window in the living room and looked out at where her house had stood for so many years. At the back of the lot, cats still scurried through all that was left of the jungle of weeds and flowers, and birds hurriedly took flight. Then Aimée turned to me and asked if I'd come with her into the backyard. Not much of an invitation: to step next door into a ruined garden, I thought, but why not? It's not every night I get asked out by a classy gal. Not many like her around, that's for sure.

So we opened the back door and carefully edged by the wrecks of the cars that lined the driveway until we reached the lane. Holding hands, we strolled into the high grass. There was the smell of jasmine and wild roses. And above us, the moonlight rained down upon the gaping hole in the earth. While the cats searched in vain for their house that had disappeared and for their familiar lookout on the carport roof, I could have almost sworn I heard wild canaries singing somewhere.

"I hope you don't mind my dragging you out here," she said.

"It's beautiful," I replied. I felt her hand gently squeeze mine. "Don't ever leave me," I said.

"Well, just don't ever do something silly — like going off to Mexico with someone else."

We stayed out there till it got real dark, and Aimée said she had to get back to the house to see that Jeremy was properly settled in. And later that night, after she fed the cats, she played for over an hour on the harpsichord.

The World Beaters

So how can Jimmy be a success when he didn't achieve anything? I mean, isn't that the way with all these flops? They're supposed to be world beaters, but they only end up beating themselves. Now that Jimmy is dead, his sister Christine in Winnipeg wants a big funeral with a minister and everything. What for? To make sure he's dead? And she isn't even his sister. Not even his half-sister. Wish I'd known that when I married him fifty-odd years ago. Would have saved the both of us a lot of trouble.

I was only nineteen then, but I'd had my eye on Jimmy for over a year. He was going into second-year engineering, and he and his mother and his little sister, Christine, lived right next door to the mayor's house in Norwood. His mother had gotten married a second time, when Jimmy was only three, to the owner of an insurance agency. But that new dad of his was already sixty years old and would die of a stroke a dozen years later. What I didn't know then was that the insurance agency had died with him, and the family was just scraping by. But they sure fooled everyone with that enormous three-storey house that had a screened-in verandah, bay windows and a huge backyard.

Still, it was nothing compared to the house next door. What a palace the mayor's house was, with pillars at the front door, a circular driveway, flowerbeds in both the frontyard and the backyard, and a massive hedge to keep prying eyes from seeing much more. Except I once strolled in bold as brass, if you please, round to the back of the house, right past those massive bay windows and everything, and saw the swimming pool and wrought-iron furniture on the patio and swaying wicker swing suspended from an oak tree in the backyard. This is for me, I thought. I'll even settle for living next door to this. For the first little while, anyway! I was tempted, really tempted, to go even further and ring the front doorbell and demand a guided tour round the house. But then I thought, well, that will have to wait. And dammit, I'm still waiting.

Jimmy's first dad had been a construction engineer and was known in the neighborhood as Big Al Adair — even though he was a small guy. He came from a wealthy family in New York and was the first world beater I'd ever heard of. Before he knew that he was to become a father, he'd died from bad liquor on a construction site in Regina. Jimmy, it seemed, would be the heir apparent. Or so everyone thought at the time. Only his mother knew what was up.

But what did I know? In any case, I never was one to waste any time. Neither was Jimmy for that matter. We hadn't been going out for more than three months when I discovered I was pregnant. And what was Jimmy's response? "Well, that calls for a beer." And he went to the icebox to get a couple of bottles.

"But what will we do?"

"Well, first, I'm going to finish this beer," he said, leaning back into the luxurious folds of his mother's best chesterfield.

"And then what?" I asked.

"What?"

"What *after* the beer?" I was getting kind of mad.

"Here's what" — and he snatched an envelope from the marble-top table and scrawled across the back: *Abigail and I have gone to get married!* And we went out to the backyard so he could tack the note onto the back door of the garage, where his mother couldn't help but see it when she came back from shopping.

I should have suspected things might go wrong when we had to take a streetcar to City Hall.

That year was a nightmare, let me tell you. We lived in a single room in an attic, and when the baby was born Jimmy couldn't study. Then he'd be off with the guys to have a beer, while I was left washing the diapers in the basement. That witch, his mother, wouldn't give us a cent. Could you believe it? My family had to pay for everything: for that room, for the baby's things, and — damn it — even for Jimmy's beer. Hell, Jimmy would have had them paying for his condoms, too, if I'd let him. Still, I figured there'd eventually be a reconciliation between him and his mother.

But that spring he failed his exams and dropped out of engineering. I guess I shouldn't have screamed at him so often when he was trying to study in the evenings, and the baby sure didn't help by waking us up in the middle of the night all the time. So off we went to a hydro project in northern Manitoba — the first of many construction sites we lived on during the next five years. Then it was up to the Yukon and the interior of BC. Jimmy even worked at a gold mine in Yellowknife. Then off to Labrador to work at a hydro project and to Newfoundland for God-knows-what. Some tunnel, I think. I can't remember. I blotted it out. We lived in every damn thing during the Depression: cabins, hotels, barracks, even tents. Wherever there was a job. As for Vincent, he got left with my parents in Winnipeg — though all the while Jimmy was working, he did send them money to look after the kid, I'll say that for him.

Those were the days when Jimmy really took to drinking. Off he'd go with the guys in the evening and about two in the morning their car would roar up to the tent and I'd hear them shouting to one other.

"See you at work."

"You bet. Provided I can see by then."

And the next day it would be the same thing. After supper the guys would arrive full of wisecracks, and Jimmy would laugh, "Sure, why not? I'm game. Let's go tie one on."

Hours later, I'd still be awake when the motor would roar again, tires would kick up stones against the tent, and then Jimmy would stagger in smelling of booze and perfume.

What a super catch! I said to myself.

And when the job was done, we were off to God-knows-where. Over those five years, I got to see a good part of the country growing up around us. Jimmy did anything and everything: labourer, truck driver, carpenter, payroll accountant and, once in a while, even foreman.

He knew enough about engineering to read the construction plans and keep the men going once they'd started.

Still, I thought, one of these days his witch of a mother has got to come through. And in December of that fifth year — when we had returned to Manitoba so Jimmy could work at a hydro project at Grand Rapids — she finally did. I can still recall tearing open that tiny envelope. It had big news. Jimmy's grandfather, Pop Adair, had died on December 3rd in New York, at the age of eighty. There was a newspaper clipping enclosed: BUSINESS TYCOON DIES OF HEART ATTACK. And to celebrate there was an invitation to Christmas dinner. Some dinner.

We got through most of the meal alright, with Jimmy talking mostly about all the big important jobs he'd been supervising lately. So when he finally got up enough nerve to ask, "Look, Mom, I could use a bit of help starting in January," she was flabbergasted.

"So could your sister and me, Jimmy. In fact, I was hoping you'd help us out. I haven't even paid last year's taxes on the house yet. I haven't even paid for this dinner. Must owe the grocer almost a hundred dollars by now."

"How's that?" I blurted out.

"Well, just why do you think people don't pay their bills?" the old witch said, staring me straight in the eye.

"I don't get it," said Jimmy. "Dad was in line to inherit more than just a few bucks from his pop in New York. And now some of that money should be coming to us. I was hoping you would have heard by now. Hardly anyone knows our address — it's always changing."

"You're *sure* you haven't heard from the Adairs, Jimmy? They seemed to like you well enough, even though your dad's parents never did take to me. There was a nasty row between Big Al and his dad when we got married. Then, when Big Al died from bad bootleg liquor in Regina, I was the one they blamed. What was I supposed to do, living in a hotel room while he went off to the construction site each day? Your dad not getting back till midnight — and even later."

"I know the feeling," I snapped.

Jimmy looked startled. "I thought they'd made up shortly after I was born. I know they were upset when Dad died the way he did. But when you wrote Pop about me being born, they came out on the train from New York with gifts and everything. Later, you know, you showed me some of their letters. So what happened?"

"Finish your cheesecake, first, Jimmy. And you, Abigail, you want a second piece?" That old witch sure knew how to make you squirm.

"Thanks," I said, "don't mind if I do." Wasn't going to let her see the torment I was going through just waiting to hear what she had to say. But Jimmy couldn't hold out against her.

"I remember those letters were wild with excitement. They'd thought they'd lost their only son forever and then they discovered I'd been born six months after Dad died."

"Oh, they came out, alright. But they were of a suspicious nature. Same as Big Al. Hired a detective and everything."

"A detective? What for?" I asked.

"More coffee, anyone? Christine, fill Jimmy's cup."

"I don't get it, Mom. Why the detective?"

"Why do you think?"

I could see Jimmy would never figure it out, but I had — or thought I had. "Because they wanted to be sure, Jimmy, that you were Big Al's son."

"Oh, you are clever. Always knew she was clever, Jimmy."

"Yeah, that's why I married her," he said, sounding like a fool.

"Oh, we all know why you married her."

That witch — she sure doesn't let up.

"Was there ever any doubt," Jimmy asked, "about Big Al being my father?"

"Oh, there were many doubts."

"There were? Just what did the detective find out?"

"Well, for one thing," and here she looked at me with that mischievous look on her face, "he found out that Big Al couldn't possibly have been your father."

"Why not?"

"Because he checked in Regina and Winnipeg — must have cost a pretty penny! — and discovered that I hadn't been pregnant before you were born. Not at all. Not even a wee bit."

"I don't get it," said Jimmy.

And neither did I, for that matter. I may have wondered if Big Al wasn't Jimmy's father. But I'd never had any doubts about who his mother was.

"Did I ever mention my friend, Judy Crabtree? Her father was a minister. No, I guess I wouldn't have. She lives in Portage la Prairie now."

"Not that I can remember." Jimmy looked puzzled.

We were the best of friends all through high school. And when I came back to Winnipeg after Big Al died, I discovered Judy was pregnant. She didn't want the baby and I . . . well . . . I decided maybe that was one way I could make Big Al's family back in New York sit up and take notice."

"What are you saying?" Jimmy asked.

But I knew what she was saying alright. My marriage and these last five years with Jimmy and Vincent had been a big mistake. That's what she was saying.

"Now, Jimmy, I don't want you to go racing off to see Judy Crabtree in Portage. She'll be terrified to death. She's married now, has a family and everything."

That was some Christmas present, let me tell you. At first Jimmy was so wild I just barely managed to convince him not to go rocketing down the highway to Portage that very night. "Think I'll have a beer," he said at last in that wry way of his, and so he stayed up in that big three-storey barn of a house till early morning and got roaring drunk instead.

And what did his so-called mother do? Stayed up with him. The two of them roaring with laughter as she recalled every detail of the phone calls to New York, the arrival of the detective, the discovery that Judy Crabtree was Jimmy's mother — "the whole kit and caboodle," as Jimmy would say. I'd gone to bed hours before, but didn't get a moment's sleep in that third-storey bedroom with laughter erupting through the house all night long.

The next day Jimmy did go off to Portage la Prairie alright. I didn't know what to expect — but, as always with Jimmy, it wasn't much. He was back by five that afternoon.

"Did you find her?" I asked.

"First, let's have a beer," he replied in that maddening way of his.

"What did she say?"

"Isn't there any beer colder than this? Look behind the milk. That's it. Good."

"Don't tell me you two spent the afternoon drinking beer?"

"Nope. Didn't spend any time at all with her. As soon as she found out who I was, she took a deep breath and backed away a step or two. Just stared at me. Then she snapped: 'You have a nerve coming here. Get the hell out! My husband will be back any minute.' And she pushed me out the door and slammed it in my face. Some way for a minister's daughter to behave! Stared out the window all the while I was getting back into the car, too. Just to make sure I didn't hang around."

The next day, after spending a few hours with Vincent at my parents' place, we left for Grand Rapids. And what a long and rotten drive that was. God knows how I put up with him and his friends for the next seven years — or why. Fortunately, the War had broken out in 1939, and there were all kinds of construction jobs: working on the airforce base in Newfoundland, munitions factories in Ontario and Quebec, and army camps all over the place. Maybe I hung around because he kept acting as if he came from a well-to-do family, as if he was always expecting important things around him to happen, as if he really was a world beater and not the flop I'd married. It was the way he had of turning to you, of snapping a question out — as if there were all kinds of hidden reserves he could tap into.

But by the time Vincent was fifteen, I'd had enough. And when I saw this ad for someone with hotel experience to work at the Hilton Hotel in Nassau, I wrote off like a shot — and let them guess later how much or how little hotel experience I had. Just another piece of fiction to splice my life together with. Luckily, my parents had recently moved to Toronto and wanted to keep Vincent with them. Suddenly I was single once more. It wasn't like before I met Jimmy, but when you're thirty-five and single, you'll settle for almost anything. And during the next eight years in the Bahamas, I pretty well did.

Meanwhile, Jimmy kept going from job to job. God, he must have known every construction company in the country! My mother wrote me that when he came to Vincent's sixteenth birthday — my first year in Nassau — he pulled up in a big shiny Chrysler and brought along an automatic phonograph and radio for a present. Well, I thought, not one of the hot shots I've been saddled up with in back seats has had a Chrysler. Maybe Jimmy isn't a dead loss after all. Still, all the while I was here, I left no stone unturned looking for some likely prospect. But — God! — some of the things I turned up beneath those stones.

So after eight years, it was back to Toronto and a job at the Hilton there. As for Jimmy, he was at some mine in Timmins. Asbestos, I think. Would have served him right to be working in the darkness, buried down there by the month. But what did I hear when he showed up the next year for Vincent's birthday?

"Think I'll settle in Timmins, Abigail."

"And what's in Timmins?"

"A pretty gal by the name of Sandy."

"You never were one for small towns, Jimmy. You know that."

"Why, I must have lived in every small town in the country, Abigail. Say, where can a guy get a drink around this joint, anyway?"

"Mom and Dad don't approve of liquor, Jimmy. You know that."

"Scared a bit of booze might make them come to life, eh?"

"And put out that cigarette, Jimmy. They don't like smoke in their house, either."

"God, with parents like those two, no wonder you're . . . "

"No wonder . . . what?"

"Think I'd better mosey on back to Timmins."

"Yes, you do that."

So off he went to his little tramp in Timmins. But later I heard that didn't work out for him either. She'd been married once and had an eight-year-old son and perhaps that was the only male she really wanted in her life. Or else she didn't take kindly to his arriving late at night smelling of beer and someone else's perfume. Or maybe he did behave himself for a change. Maybe she was the one running after whoever would offer to care for her and her son in exchange for a quick tumble in bed. Every well-heeled trucker or construction worker passing through town could have been a candidate. Would have served Jimmy right.

Frankly, I don't know how anyone could have stood him then, except for that sister of his back in Winnipeg. She'd gotten married a few years back and had a couple of kids of her own. Jimmy used to drive out to meet them all whenever they came camping out this way: Niagara Falls, Stratford, even some fishing village in New England.

Seems they liked him well enough, though I don't know why.

But he didn't come back to Toronto. And I didn't hear anything about him for years. Then one March — Vincent must have been about twenty-nine then — the phone rang and it was Jimmy telling Vincent not to be surprised if he dropped by one day soon and could they go off to a pub together? This time, I thought, Jimmy will be the one in for a surprise. Vincent was now engaged to a mousy little girl whose family were all teetotallers. Even I could get feeling parched after half an hour in their company. Hell, even my parents could!

Sure enough, in less than a month Jimmy was back in Toronto and working on the extension to the subway line. Didn't see him often, but at Vincent's wedding I could see Jimmy puzzling at his new in-laws. And you can imagine how they returned his gaze once he asked them, "Say, where can a guy get a beer around this joint?"

The next dozen years must have convinced him of the worst. Vincent named their baby Eustace after his father-in-law and settled down in a new suburb only twenty minutes from where he worked as an engineer for the city. I could see that Jimmy was proud Vincent had become the engineer he'd never been, but he was puzzled, too. Vincent just didn't have the time of day for Jimmy. Neither did his wife, Prue.

Jimmy was now into his early sixties and was no longer finding it easy to get on at new construction sites.

But then, at last, Jimmy's ship seemed to have come in. Vincent phoned and I could tell at once from his voice that he was impressed.

"Dad's got a job — in Algeria."

"What's he going to do there, beside drinking beer? Wait a minute. They won't even *let* him drink beer in that part of the world."

"He's going to work for an oil company."

"You'd think they'd have more sense than to hire an old crock like your dad."

"He'll be earning close to a thousand dollars a week — and he gets two paid vacations to anywhere in North America or Europe every year."

I could sense that at last he felt really proud of his dad. "When does this job begin?"

"They'll be flying him out in three weeks. He sure won't have much time to pack up his apartment and sell the car. Dad was saying that next Christmas maybe Prue and I could fly out to see him there, if her parents would look after the kids."

"I wouldn't run out to buy the tickets just yet, Vincent."

"Dad said he'd buy us the tickets with his first paycheck."

No point in going on, I knew. Jimmy always had expected something big to enter his life and this was it. Well, about time! And the last person he'd want to see would be me.

From Vincent I heard about Jimmy selling off his fancy Chrysler and moving out of his apartment. Most of the stuff got stored with Vincent. And then he was gone. Nothing. Not a word. Not for weeks. When I did think of him, I imagined him out in the desert wearing one of those pith helmets and asking, "Say, where's the nearest bar around here anyway? Let's go tie one on." If he was lucky, there wouldn't be any takers.

Any day I expected to hear that a letter from Jimmy had arrived with the air tickets. But when Vincent did hear, it was from right here in Toronto. Like every other windfall in his life, that job turned out to be a mirage. Jimmy was at St. Joseph's Hospital. He'd been found the month before wandering the streets, not sure where he was. A streetcar conductor had had to slam on the brakes to keep from running him down.

Days before he was to leave for Algeria, he had to go in for a medical, and that's when it was discovered there was trouble with his kidneys and liver. All that beer had finally caught up with him. And that was not all. Veins and arteries leading to his legs had almost rotted through. Rotted through or blocked up, I never did get the story straight. Anyway, they were causing him a lot of pain.

"Just call me the bionic man," Jimmy laughed when we visited him at the hospital. "All sorts of plastic tubes in there now. Gee, Vincent, you forgot to bring along a six-pack like I asked you to."

The city got him an apartment at a nominal rent in a public housing complex in Cabbage Town, and when Vincent and I went to visit him we did bring him a case of beer. Same old Jimmy, I could see. But when we went for a walk in the park nearby, he had to stop every dozen yards or so.

"Damn pain. Starts up and if you ignore it — wow! — you sure pay."

He wanted us all to go back to his apartment. Once there he said: "Watch this" and stepped onto the balcony to throw bread out for the pigeons. Those birds just swarmed into the air as soon as they heard the door opening. When they saw the bread, they'd wheel and circle, swoop and dive, till you thought you were in the sky as well.

He seemed happy enough and so after that first visit we just forgot him. Except on his grandson's birthday, when Jimmy would appear with a gift he couldn't afford. Just like him. Like a ghost from the past. And you could see him pursing his lips as if smoking a cigarette when he caught sight of Prue's parents looking at him in that way that even makes me feel queasy. Before too long, he'd go outside to have a smoke and then forget to come back in. After a few years he didn't even bother showing up anymore.

Serves him right. No girl from Timmins will ever have him now, I thought. And then one day — in the summer of '85 — Vincent, Prue and I were downtown at the Silver Rail when I heard Jimmy's voice in that famous battle cry of his. "Say, can't a fellow get a drink at this joint?" And sure enough there he was at a table with two well-dressed young men, each with an almost empty glass in his hand. "Christine's kids, Mark and Joel," he explained when Vincent and I came up to their table, "from Winnipeg."

"Will you be staying long in Toronto?" Vincent asked.

"We've moved here," Mark said.

"Mark and Joel are staying at my place for a few days till they get an apartment. Mark's interning at North York Branson and Joel is articling for the Crown."

The table was littered with glasses and dishes. They must have just packed away a meal that would make the check at least three pages long. And those two nephews of Jimmy's were still ordering! A pair of spendthrifts, just like their uncle. Must run in the family. Now how did that happen?

"Uncle Jimmy, why don't you try the Czechoslovakian beer on the menu?" suggested Mark helpfully.

"Or there's this Japanese beer. Sapporo, I know, is pretty good." Joel was not to be outdone.

You could see they made Jimmy feel like a king, so we left them to their festivities. What they were celebrating, God only knows. Jimmy must have known by then that he didn't have much time left.

But still I was surprised when the nurse at St. Joseph's phoned three months later to say Jimmy had passed away that morning. It seemed sadder because it was Christmas Day.

Later, I heard from one of the orderlies, when I came to the hospital to collect some of his things, that the night before he died his two nephews had come over with presents and, of course, some booze. And then, as if that weren't bad enough, they'd shut the door and held a party. It created an uproar, and one of the nurses on the bed with Jimmy had gotten fired. Well, I thought, he died the way he lived, drunk in bed with a tart.

Then that sister of his, Christine, phoned from Winnipeg to say she would be flying in after Christmas for the funeral.

"There's no money for a funeral service," I explained. *In fact, there's never been enough money for anything!* I felt like screaming. There was a pause at the other end of the line before she said, "I'll pay for the service."

"But Jimmy was not a religious person."

"How would you know?"

"A service could cost $3000 — and I don't know when you'll ever be paid back. It could be months before whatever he left behind is probated."

"I'll wait."

"But don't you see it's hypocritical to spend that kind of money when a cremation costs only $999 at the Windy Hill Crematorium here."

Christine paused for a moment. "Well, that's settled," I thought.

But she wasn't about to give in that easily. "I do not want my brother incinerated like so much garbage," she declared in that flat way of hers that reminded me of her mother.

But Jimmy liked smoking, I felt like replying. Then I thought I'd better not.

So there was nothing for it. In early January, Christine flew in and the two nephews came to the funeral. They even brought some friends from work. There must have been $200 worth of flowers getting frozen at the graveside. And the coffin — some dark, shiny wood, mahogany I think, with carved handles — housed Jimmy better than he'd ever been housed in his life.

Then the minister spouted a bunch of lies about what a prince of a man Jimmy had been and how well-loved by everyone — especially by his two nephews. I didn't even feel guilty at not inviting Christine and her sons and their friends back for tea. After all, they did have cars to find their own way back to wherever it was they belonged.

So they all roared off still prattling about what a fine service it had been, the girls reeking of perfume, if you can believe it. Wouldn't surprise me if they were going off to have a beer at Jimmy's old haunt, the Silver Rail. What cheek! I could see that Vincent was upset — he kept staring back at the grave and then at the road they'd vanished down.

Made me wonder at the way Jimmy's mother might have felt when she read his note that afternoon we ran off to get married at City Hall.

"Forgive Me, Father, for I Have Sinned," She Said

Well, I hope Joseph's pleased. He has only himself to blame if he's not — along with those friends of his from Canada. Certainly, until they arrived, I was willing to carry on with our married life together a while longer. As for Roger, he wasn't all that anxious to bring matters to a head, that's for sure. Instead he seemed content to remain invisible — and uncommitted — forever.

So when those friends of Joseph's phoned from London that fateful Thursday, I sensed the entire weekend would be a disaster. Friday was the beginning of the Easter break. The children were looking forward to their holiday, and by noon Joseph would be through teaching here at Liverpool College. We had already promised to take the kids up to Shap, in the Lake Country. But I had been planning another one of my migraines for Friday morning — just before we were to head off in the Renault.

For a change, Roger and I could have spent the whole weekend together at his place. Uninterruptedly. Roger teaches ethics in the Philosophy Department at the University of Liverpool. He's always going off someplace or other where they're short of ethics: London, Oxford, Paris. And he's always wanting me to go with him. Why, once he even took me with him to Vienna. Now that really took some explaining to Joseph. The trips closer to home, I insisted, were to see girlfriends or my cousin in Manchester, do a bit of sightseeing or hear public lectures. But Vienna? Now Joseph was more than puzzled; he was suspicious. But Vienna it was. Roger was to meet me in the departure lounge at the airport, and once I'd waved goodbye to Joseph and the kids, I knew Roger and I were home free. But that's another story.

This story concerns that fateful weekend when Joseph's Canadian friends arrived. I phoned Roger early Friday morning. "We're all supposed to be meeting in the Lake Country for the weekend, Roger. Joseph's even arranged for us to pick them up at the railway station at Penrith. There's nothing I can do."

"Tell Joseph you've got another one of your migraines."

"I'd plannned to, but I can't. He wants to show me off to his friends."

"Tell him you'll meet them back in Liverpool. Tell him you don't like the Lake Country."

"But he bought that cottage because I said I loved the Lake Country. We've nothing like it back in Canada."

"Tell him you've had a change of heart."

"Roger, you'll just have to wait."

"Wait? Cindy, we haven't seen each other for almost a week."

"And just as well. I must have been mad to let you come over to the house last Tuesday. And to carry on as we did, on that couch in front of the livingroom window

— even if the curtains were drawn — why, that was madness."

"But such a divine madness."

"Well, if you hadn't dilly-dallied forever, I wouldn't have been quite so frantic. But you — you wanted to try everything. And there was Fred in the livingroom with us, growling, then rolling his eyes and gasping for breath. I thought he was going to have a fit when you got us all tied up in knots that last time."

"And how do you think I felt? I expected that dog to take a nip out of my hindquarters at any moment."

"Would have served you right!"

"I still don't see why we couldn't just have shut him outside."

"Because he would have set up a howl that would've been heard throughout the neighbourhood."

"All the more reason to continue this weekend from where we left off."

"Sorry, Roger, but I know it won't work. This weekend you'll just have to cuddle up with another one of your lectures. Perhaps you can call it 'Bedside Ethics'."

"Not a bad title, but I'd have to do more research first. Suppose I come up to the Lake Country. I'll take a room at one of the inns in Penrith."

"Don't you dare!"

"Just keep your eye peeled for a sporty blue Jaguar."

"Roger, please, you mustn't."

But when he finally rang off, nothing had been settled, and there were other, more immediate, matters to attend to. I didn't waste much time, believe me, in throwing our clothes into shopping bags, along with some bread, peanut butter and a can of beans. Remember the picnic basket, I told myself. But keep the rubbers in the bottom drawer of the dresser in case Joseph does agree to toodle off to the Lake Country without me.

When he came home, though, right after giving his Victorian Lit. class, and I had collapsed in tears with my migraine on the sofa, what does he do but make a scene? I have never known him to be so disagreeable.

"Joseph, I simply can't move with my head splitting apart."

"You were moving quickly enough yesterday when you headed into town to that ethics tutorial at the university."

"That was yesterday."

"Just pretend you're off to another tutorial — at the Lake Country this time."

"But I'm not in a philosophical frame of mind today."

"I couldn't give a goddamn. Get off that sofa. Now! Do you hear?"

"No need to shout. You'll alarm all the neighbors with your bellowing. Look, there's your department head — just passed by the livingroom window. A few minutes later and who knows what he might have seen? Dr. Joseph Crosswell beating up on Mrs. Crosswell perhaps? That's one of the disadvantages, isn't it dear, of living in a Staff House right on campus. Why, it almost outweighs the major advantage — you can go on toadying up to your superiors all day long."

"Cindy, why do we always have to fight?"

"Oh, alright. I'll go to that stupid stone cottage with you and the kids. But not before I go to mass tonight."

"Tonight?"

"Let's not forget it was your idea that I become a Catholic. Don't blame me if I've become devout. It's all your doing."

"You can go to mass in Penrith."

"In Penrith? But I was looking forward to a chat with Father Donnelly."

"Cindy, we're leaving in an hour. We're already late."

It would serve his friends right if they had to sit around forever in that massive stone waiting room at the railway station. Mind you, Joseph did move much faster than I expected in getting everything packed away into the Renault minivan. Luckily, I just had time to tuck the rubbers into my purse and phone Roger to tell him that the weekend was definitely off.

For the first half hour it was pretty grim, let me tell you, but then once we were onto the M57, with cars whizzing by on all sides, I couldn't help but laugh at the thought of Roger's Jaguar being one of them.

"You were quite right, Joseph, I'm feeling better already."

"Sorry to have snapped at you back there, Luv."

"All my fault. We'll have a marvellous weekend. Let's play a game, children."

"Can Fred play, too?" asked Andrew.

"That depends."

"On what?" asked Jenny.

"On whether he can guess what I spy with my little eye."

"What do you spy, Mum?"

And so the game began: "Is it a *j*acket?" "A *j*eep?" "The *j*unction?" "A *j*et?" "A *j*ogger?"

And although none of the children are slow and even Joseph tried his damnedest, luckily no one spotted the blue Jaguar that raced ahead of us on the road to Penrith.

I could see that Joseph's spirits were lifting, so I thought, yes, now is the time to strike. "Don't forget I want to stop off at the church in Penrith."

"Oh, give us a rest, Mum," piped up Ron.

"I won't be long. You can pick up your friends at the railway station, get all unpacked at the cottage, and by the time you get back, I'll be ready."

"Oh, now be reasonable, Luv. Not even my Aunt Mary, who became a nun at sixteen, spends as much time in front of the altar as you."

But I could see that he was smiling, and so when we got to Penrith, he drove straight to the church.

"Sure we can't pick you up right after we've collected our friends at the railway station?"

"But Joseph, you know it will be quite a sqeeze to get us all into the car together. You'll have to come back for their luggage anyway. Besides, there are some things you just can't rush. I need some time. To be alone with my thoughts."

"What thoughts?" snapped Jenny.

"What things?" inquired Patrick, peering into the almost empty shopping bag of food.

"We're always rushing," added Ron.

"Just keep it up, children, and I'll have another one of my migraines."

"Leave your mother alone, you lot. She's right. There isn't enough room in the minivan. I'll be back around seven to collect you, Luv."

But just when I thought I was scot-free, the dog spotted Roger parked in his Jaguar at the side of the church, and started rolling his eyes and gasping for breath.

"What's wrong with Fred, Mum?"

"You'd better get him to the railway station right away and give him a long run. I expect he's been cooped up too long."

As soon as the van turned the corner, Roger swung the Jaguar round in front of the church and less than ten minutes later we were up the stairs and into his room above the pub at the corner. Trust Roger. I just knew he'd never take no for an answer.

And once that door was shut, he didn't. In that hour and a half, the trumpets blared, the heavens opened and the angels sang — or something like that. Then I had to dash back to the church where Joseph would be picking me up.

"Forgive me, Father, for I have sinned," I blurted out as soon as I'd collapsed into the confessional.

"Are they sins of the spirit or of the flesh?"

Well, there was nothing for it, was there? Anyway, I didn't figure I'd be back anytime soon, so I told him everything.

"How often?" the voice interrupted with a gasp.

"I've already told you. Two or three times a week. For the last year."

"With just one man?"

"Isn't that enough?"

"And before you moved to Liverpool?"

"I met Roger in Lincolnshire when he came to visit his mum. Joseph had been out of a job for over six months and he was so upset that, finally, at Christmas, he became impotent. Some Christmas present, let me tell you. Joy to the world! That's when Roger appeared on the scene. Just in the nick of time."

"Have you thought of your children?" His words sounded like a stock response he'd picked up from *The Family Counselling Book for Parish Priests*.

"Of course I've thought of them," I snapped. "It's not as if I'd just picked up and left Joseph and the kids."

From the strangled sounds behind the screen, I could tell that hadn't gone over too well. "Look, Father, I can't wait around forever while you mull this over. Joseph will be along in a few minutes to collect me. So you think about it carefully and consult your books, and tell me, when I come back tomorrow evening, what you've decided I should do."

"But wait . . . " he began.

"Tomorrow evening," I repeated, and I was out of the confessional just in time to see Joseph come wandering into the church to look for me.

The priest had come dashing out as well, but seeing me with Joseph stopped him dead in his tracks. His eyes were rolling and now he was the one gasping for breath.

"Come on, Cindy. Supper's getting cold. Was there a big queue tonight or what?"

"Not really. But it's good you came in when you did. I was talking that poor man's ear off."

"Well, he didn't look bored."

The next morning I'd planned to meet Roger again at the King's Head Tavern, but when I woke up I was furious to discover it was almost noon.

Joseph and the children had taken Michael and Christine for a walk to the stone quarry before breakfast, and they were famished by the time they returned.

What was I supposed to do? This time I really was getting a migraine, and so I let Joseph look after the food he'd bought. Then I grabbed the picnic basket and we were off in the Renault to show our guests the sights. But wouldn't you know it? In Penrith, the dog again caught sight of Roger, who was getting into his car outside the inn, and immediately Fred started to go into the same routine again.

I waited till we'd turned the corner before I dared say anything. "Joseph, do you think Fred's alright? His eyes are rolling and he looks as if he's about to have a fit. There's no room for him to breathe back there." But I might just as well have not said a thing; Joseph's attention was all on the road. And Roger, who would have hung on my every word, was already blocks away. As the car picked up speed, I really got mad. "Joseph, stop the car! At once, do you hear?"

"We can't stop here, my Luv, or we'll all be killed."

The thought of Roger getting into his Jaguar vanished as a huge lorry bore down on us. The next moment it roared by in a way that made the road tremble and the houses shake. Fred was so astonished that he snapped out of his fit. The children, too, were deathly quiet.

"Sorry, Joseph." Might as well be a good sport, I thought. There's just no chance of my seeing Roger this afternoon anyway. And Joseph's Canadian friends must be getting a little miffed at the way I've been ignoring them ever since we arrived in the Lake Country.

"Michael, how long is it since you last saw Joseph?"

"About fifteen years."

"Much too long. Now we have to make up for lost time. This afternoon let's go to all our favourite places, Joseph."

"We can't go to *all* our favourite places, Luv. That would take at least a week."

"I know, just let's go to that hill where we camped on our honeymoon."

In answer, Joseph floored the gas pedal and off we went. Fred barked, the children whooped, and the car flung up stones as we turned up a steep incline. We parked the car and ran up a winding path to the top of the place we call "Honeymoon Point". New perspectives opened at every turn — lakes, villages, valleys emerged briefly from the mist and then vanished again.

"Here's our magic spot," said Jenny, as she spread out the blanket.

"Yes," agreed Patrick, putting down the picnic basket.

"A splendid place for a honeymoon, I must say," Christine laughed.

But then Patrick opened the picnic basket. And there were my aspirins and Perrier water. And nothing else.

"Oh, Mum," gasped Jenny. "Not again."

"Now you know I can't think of everything. Why didn't someone remind me about the thermos and peanut butter and bread?"

"Don't worry. It's *your* turn to be our guests anyway," said Michael. "We can eat later, but first let's explore where this path leads." The children shouted their agreement and tore through the bush ahead of Michael and Christine.

So off I trudged after them. There was nothing for it, was there? But I'd had no breakfast, and if we had to walk for hours I just knew my head would start to split open with each step. By the time I'd caught up with them, they'd actually climbed to a lookout post on the other side of the hill and were gazing down over a valley. Below, through the mist, you could just see a river winding by a farmhouse and fields covered with sheep. Soon the pounding in my head would be intolerable.

"Joseph, it's all my fault, I know, but this is impossible. I'm going back to the car. I'm sorry. When does mass in Penrith begin tonight, do you know?"

"No need to rush." Christine touched my shoulder as if I were a child who had to be consoled.

But I had had enough. "Can't you see how miserable everyone is, Joseph? How can you insist that we go on?"

But insist they did. So that by the time we'd tramped up hill and down dale, and eaten at the restaurant half way down the hill, and then taken the dog for a run, and finally gotten back to the cottage for a late supper — well, there just wasn't time to get off to mass at Penrith that evening. And I felt just furious when I thought of poor Roger all by himself in that cold damp room above the pub.

We spent the evening, if you can believe it, walking along the road and speculating how long it would have taken farmers hereabouts to collect all the stones from their fields to make the fences that cut in all directions through the landscape.

That night, as I fell asleep, I could hear the rain starting up. The end to a perfect day. And in the morning the rain was coming down even harder. Everyone else in the cottage was still asleep when we got up, dressed and had breakfast. Joseph finally had to admit it had been a mistake to have our guests meet us in the Lake Country. It was lucky we'd brought so few things, but even so there was no way, with our guests and their luggage, that we'd all get into the minivan. So Joseph and I nipped down to Penrith in the Renault, and I let him off on the outskirts of the town to hitchhike his way back to Liverpool. He didn't have to wait long, believe me. There was a general exodus starting up that morning. I waited at a lay-by till I saw a Toyota pick him up and then I was off like a shot to Roger's. But — worse luck — would you believe it? No car. No Roger. I could have wept.

So back to the cottage it was to pack up everybody for the ride to Liverpool. I could see that Michael and Christine were astonished that I would have sent Joseph off by himself in the rain, but what else was I to do? Anyway, that wasn't the first time Joseph's had to hitchhike home that way. There were other occasions, usually when Joseph had made me angry, and I had decided to stay on with the children for an extra week.

But wouldn't you know it? Once we all got packed into the minivan — Michael in front, Christine wedged in back with the children, and Fred at the very back with the luggage — the sun came out, the mist started to retreat from the lakes and hills, and in fact it was one of those days in the Lake Country when fields, rivers and farms all fold into one another until you'd swear the landscape was alive.

And then I remembered. "I'm sorry, everyone, but I'm afraid I forgot to pack a lunch. But we can stop at a restaurant I know just outside of Liverpool."

"Oh, Mum, I reminded you," called Jenny from the back seat.

"I intended to remember, dear. But I forgot."

"You always forget," snapped Ron.

"Now don't be rude."

"She forgets everything but mass. Won't ever forget that, oh, no."

But then Michael surprised me. "Don't you kids like restaurants?" he asked.

"Not when we always have to order what's cheapest on the menu."

"So this time order what's most expensive on the menu. My treat."

"He's joking!" whispered Ron.

"I don't think so," Jenny said.

"Cor blimey!" concluded Patrick in his best Cockney accent. "The second time in two days."

"I can't let you pay for all our meals," I said unconvincingly.

"Not *all* of them," he laughed. "Besides, we expect Joseph to have dinner ready by the time we arrive in Liverpool."

So off we toodled down the road, all of us a merry crew now. Except maybe for Christine, who was awfully quiet wedged in the back seat.

God, I thought, looking him over where he sat beside me, Michael's just like Roger. None of this pennypinching that Joseph's so fond of, except when it comes to buying things for himself — like that £200 suit he got before we went off on that plane trip to visit my parents in Vancouver. Of course, Joseph had always wanted to drive through the Rockies, so there was nothing for it, was there? But despite the spectacular view, it wasn't much fun for the children in that old beater he'd bought.

And then we were so strapped for cash, before we got to Winnipeg, we had to sleep in the car in a Safeway parking lot. That was some occasion — with three children up hour after hour.

But Michael is like Roger. Knows how to have a good time. I sneaked a glance sideways to catch a glimpse of Michael's face, but when I glanced up again there were Christine's eyes staring at me in the rear-view mirror. Oh, well. Then I *did* turn deliberately to study his face. "Joseph's often spoken of you. You were his closest friend in Canada. I thought it was such a shame you were away when we came through in the car. All of his old buddies were gone that summer — off to some conference or other. I told Joseph he should have written beforehand."

"I was really sorry to miss him."

"One of the few, I suspect. Didn't he create something of a scandal in Winnipeg before he left — getting engaged to three different girls at once."

"He's just a very likeable person."

"And you're a very generous person. Buying us lunch day after day. What a shame I didn't get to know you sooner." All the while it was hard to tell what was uppermost in his mind: that long slit in my skirt or the other shorter one in my blouse.

Or had I gotten things all wrong? Again. Lucky Christine. She got it right the first time.

Behind us, I could hear the voices of the children mingling. Oh, they can be so sweet — when they want to be.

But what's that smell? Must be some diesel truck on the road ahead.

"Michael," Christine's voice sounded alarmed. "What is that flashing red light on the dashboard?"

Oh, God, I thought. Not again!

We screeched to a halt at a lay-by, and at once the car was engulfed in clouds of steam and burning oil. I turned off the ignition, but up front everything kept perking along anyway.

"I think we should all get out fast," announced Jenny in that maddeningly sensible way of hers. I grabbed my purse, and we all burst out of the Renault — and just in time. About us cars stopped, and people rushed up to look as Michael flung open the hood. You could have roasted an ox in the flames that leapt out of that engine. Cars passed by us with children — and adults — gazing in wonder. Finally, someone ran down to the lake with a pail, and flung the water onto the flames and billowing smoke. Then a strange thing happened. Sparks flashed, sheet lightning erupted, and there was an explosion that flung the car right up off the ground. But that was it — except for the charred smell of paint peeling off metal.

"Listen, everyone, I'll have to go phone the Royal Automobile Club for a tow truck. So you all wait here, and keep an eye on things."

"Mom," said Jenny, "don't you think this looks worse than that time in Scotland?"

"Nothing could be worse than that time in Scotland," explained Ron.

"You're sure you don't want me to go instead," offered Michael.

"I've done this before," I explained. "No trouble really. The RAC man will be along very quickly. And before he could say anything more, I put out my thumb and then my leg, and at once cars were screeching to a halt about us. A whole fleet of cars. Could have created an accident on the spot. Then, just as I was about to get into a black Bentley, I heard a familiar horn sound.

Trust Roger. Dear *splendid* Roger. He must have a sixth sense about these things. There was the blue Jaguar, and I was into it like a flash. Just had time to wave goodbye as we tore back along the road to an inn where I could phone. I really had been upset to miss Roger last night and then again this morning. But now with Joseph already halfway back to Liverpool and everybody else stranded on the highway, who was there to get in our way? The phone call at the inn took less then two minutes and it took another two minutes to rent a room — which left Roger and me almost a whole hour by ourselves.

Then it was back onto the road and in no time flat I had a ride in a grey Daimler with a middle-aged barrister from Manchester. Quite distinguished in his own way. Roger had offered to drive me, but I thought it too risky — Jenny might remember the blue Jaguar. Besides, Jack Salter and I had a lot of fun on that ride. And before he let me out he said that someone so talented should really forget ethics and study law.

I must say I was surprised when the RAC man turned out to be Mr. Dolly. Every time we break down, Mr. Dolly turns up to get us going again. Except it's not always Joseph I'm with. But whether it's Roger, or whoever, Mr. Dolly never lets on. Though not even Mr. Dolly could figure out the scene this time: Michael and Christine and the kids and me. You could see him puzzling as to the bedroom arrangements.

Then he turned his attention to the car, and he really did look morally outraged when he saw what was beneath the hood.

"Do you think it's shoddy workmanship on the part of the French?" I prompted.

When he didn't reply, I saw my opportunity and went right on. "Perhaps you could just top everything up with water and oil? We really must get going, Mr. Dolly," and I looked impatiently at my watch.

"Did you not see a red warning light flashing on the dashboard? The car, Madam, is a ruin."

"Now, Mr. Dolly, that's what you said last time, and you see here we are again." His eyes glazed over for a moment.

"Madam, I will have to phone for a lorry. As you must certainly be aware by now, this comes under the heading of a 'Removal'."

"Oh, well, if there's nothing else for it." But I did make him tow us back to the inn where Roger and I had just been dallying, and we had lunch in the restaurant while waiting for the RAC to come and collect us. The clerk behind the counter had a strange look on his face.

Michael and Christine, I must admit, were good sports and kept the children laughing throughout the meal. And Michael was as good as his word and paid for the whole lot. Lucky for me, too, because I suddenly realized that I'd forgotten my purse in the room upstairs where Roger and I had earlier spent such a busy hour.

I was wondering how I'd slip away, but when I went to the washroom, the maid who had found it met me at the door. Definitely worth the five-pound tip.

An hour later, the Renault was in the back of the lorry and we were all in the cab — on the bench behind the drivers' seat — tearing into Liverpool.

By the end of the week when we took Michael and Christine to catch the night ferry to Dublin, I was convinced that Joseph and I couldn't go on the way we had any longer. Our last evening together had been a success — Michael took us all out to dinner again — though the car, just back from its expensive stay at the garage, did get a flat, and later we all had to push when the battery went dead. But what finally put a damper on everything was the offer I made while we were saying goodbye at the dock.

"Let me know, Michael, when you're getting back, and I'll drive you and Christine to London to catch your plane."

"Cindy!"

I could see that Joseph was really surprised — and upset.

"Well, I don't see what *you're* so mad about," I said.

"This will be the third time in as many months you'll have left us to fend for ourselves — without even a car."

"But I'll be with your friends, Joseph. Your dear friends from Canada." I could see Michael and Christine were uncomfortable, but I was counting on their surprise to keep them from saying anything. Now, if only all went well, Roger and I would have the whole weekend again together in London. Enough of this rushing off to some room above an inn for just an hour or so.

But Christine surprised me. "We couldn't allow it. A drive to London is just too big a favour."

"Of course, it's not. Besides, it will give me a few days to do some shopping. I haven't shopped in London in years."

"Luv, you know you were in London just last Christmas."

"Now, you listen to me, Joseph. I'm thirty-three years old and I will not be treated like a child. Do you understand?"

But then Michael butted in. "We couldn't possibly let you drive us to London, Cindy. Besides, what if the car broke down again. We'd miss our plane."

"Oh that couldn't possibly happen," I insisted, but their look of alarm told me I wasn't too convincing. Anyway, I could see their minds were made up. And to make matters worse, when I told Roger later that the trip to London was off, what did he say but, "No use pushing our luck, Cindy. It would be a bit much to go charging off to London so soon after the trip to the Lake Country."

By now, it was obvious to me that I was just being taken for granted — by everyone. Enough of this, I thought. Time to bring matters to a head. Why should I always be treated like some impulsive fourteen-year-old? Joseph would never change. And if Roger didn't want to commit himself — well, there are other fish in the sea. And I'd been getting phone calls from one of them ever since returning from the Lake Country a few days ago. That middle-aged barrister from Manchester — the one with the grey Daimler — sure hadn't wasted any time, believe me. So the next time Roger tried to talk his way over when Joseph and the kids were at school, I let him. But Roger knew something was up, although he wasn't quite sure what.

"You alright?"

"Why shouldn't I be alright?"

"Not still upset about London?"

"Not really."

"There's a good girl," and he brushed his hand over the back of my head as if I were a pet poodle or something.

"Sure we couldn't put Fred out of the bedroom?"

I'd insisted, this time, that the couch in the living room was out of the question. "I've already told you he'll wake up the whole neighbourhood with his howling."

"Come up to my place — why don't you? — in a few days."

"Can't."

"Can't? Why not?"

"Going to Manchester. Tonight."

"Tonight? You sure don't give a fellow much warning, do you? Who's in Manchester?"

"My cousin. She's invited me."

"Oh."

At the door, before he came downstairs, he reminded me the rubber was still tangled somewhere in the bed sheets. But I told him not to worry — I'd look after that. And I did.

Before Joseph drove me off to catch the train that night, I had made sure the bedclothes were all in order — and the spent rubber was on Joseph's side of the bed. Serve him right. Let Joseph puzzle whether it was his or not. And let Roger puzzle whether he shouldn't have gone back upstairs after all and taken it away with him. Let him wonder, too, if Joseph might not be phoning him — to demand what exactly had been going on in his ethics tutorial. As for me, I wasn't going to puzzle or wonder about anything. I had my mind made up. I was going to Manchester, and I hoped my cousin would understand. It might take Joseph and Roger quite awhile to get their heads together and figure things out. But until then I'll just have to wait patiently to see if Roger phones. But if he doesn't, well that will settle matters, won't it? In the meantime, I can study law. Who knows? It might come in handy some day.

The Annunciation of Love

I should have known when the card arrived from Cindy the Friday before Thanksgiving that this year's celebration would be unlike any other I'd ever experienced. Cindy had married a friend of mine, Joseph Crosswell, who had come over from Leeds in the early Sixties to teach English at the university in Winnipeg. He'd lived in the apartment block next door and during the three years he was there I'd gotten to know him pretty well. I'd sold him some insurance and we still kept in touch, but, to put it bluntly, there was no insurance policy around for the kind of problems he had. He left in the midst of a scandal — running off with a colleague's wife, Maggie Travers. But a couple of years later I got a wedding announcement from Liverpool which declared, in no uncertain terms, that he was marrying someone else altogether, a gal by the name of Cindy.

And now this latest card, arriving more than twenty years later, was in the nature of another announcement, one that in its own way seemed to define the Sixties — or so I thought at the time. On the front of it is a photograph of Cindy in a hospital bed, but not in a hospital gown.

Instead she is wearing a pale red, see-through negligée, and in her arms is a baby, who is receiving the full impact of Cindy's fixed gaze. Devotion? Curiosity? Alarm? Fury? You cannot tell, so you open the card and there is the announcement of the birth of a baby girl, Rebecca, except the name of the father isn't that of Joseph Crosswell, but that of a total stranger. And beneath the first announcement is a second, stating that Cindy and the stranger will be getting married on Thanksgiving Day. As a kind of afterthought, squeezed in at the bottom of the card, there is a third announcement — that of Cindy and Joseph's recent divorce.

That figures, I thought. These flower children of the Sixties (still much admired by some — myself included, I suspect) will keep on with their antics as long as they've a breath left. Even the wedding of a flower child would be bound to be different. Probably with music from the Beatles playing "I Want to Hold Your Hand."

But why had she sent the card to me? Cindy and I had met only once when she and Joseph and their kids were visiting in Winnipeg — and what a disastrous encounter that had been! She must have realized that she was one flower child that I thoroughly disapproved of. So why the card? Was it a taunt? Or was she trying to justify herself in some way — or simply brazen it out? Or, more likely, was she just showing off again?

I sell insurance for the Great West Life, and the statistics I've seen on the Sixties — divorce rates, drug addictions, arrests, accidental deaths — really make me suspect that here is a generation that's still experiencing the wrath of God. More than the rest of us, anyway. Thank God, I thought, our own children went through their teens in the late Seventies. And now that we were into the Eighties, we'd put even more distance between us and that dangerous, unpredictable decade. Made me feel a bit more comfortable having that kind of insurance.

Then — out of the blue — my son, Bobby, simply dropped out of Management Studies at the University of Toronto to go to an ashram just outside of New York. And ever since he came back he's taken to chanting Hindu prayers with a vengeance. Sometimes eight hours a day! I'll wake up in the middle of the night and I'll hear him at it: *"Om. Om. Om."* Like bees humming! The sound reverberates throughout the house all the way from the basement, where he's built a little shrine. He wanted to become a Hindu priest, but they wouldn't have him, thank God. Not to the ashram born, so to speak.

I also have a younger child, Francie, who's become a computer technician. She's happily married and is going to have a baby next January. None of this having a child while you're between husbands for her. She met Warren three years ago when he came into the Centennial Library, on Donald Street, and asked at the information counter where the Russian section was. She had just asked the same question and so they got to talking about Russian poets. Then, when he came over to her place a week later, he brought along some translations of Pushkin's poems, and the next thing you know — well it was a pretty good wedding, and, unlike what Cindy has in mind, it took place before she got pregnant. I kind of like these things being kept more traditional. Makes me appear old fashioned, I know, but so what?

Anyway, on Thanksgiving Day this year I thought I'd get a bit of rest. We'd been invited over to Francie's for dinner. Though if no one says the blessing in Hindi or Russian — or anything else, for that matter — that will suit me just fine. Two of Francie's girlfriends that she's known since elementary school will be there: Melanie Williams and Jackie Jacobson. It will be good to see them again as well. But I don't know why Warren also had to invite a couple of classmates from his Russian seminar. A lot of work for Francie when she's already six months pregnant. Warren expects her to work too hard. She's been helping to put him through university so that he can get an MA in Russian and then maybe he can land a job with Foreign Affairs next March. So I'm really hopeful.

But I guess I should have sensed what was coming as soon as we got to Francie's apartment. Melanie was already there with her current boyfriend, a news editor at the *Winnipeg Free Press* who looks old enough to be her father.

"Hi, Melanie. Francie tells me you're into journalism these days."

"She's already the best columnist in the paper," said Daddy proudly. He looked to be in his middle forties. A trim build, with a smooth round face that smiled all the time. Glasses, moustache — at first glance, a thoroughly respectable appearance.. But, dammit! watch him closely and you begin to ask yourself, so what in the hell is Melanie going out with this middle-aged tomcat for?

"I don't know what I would have done if Wally hadn't been able to get me the job with the paper."

"We were lucky." Daddy sounded very enthusiastic. "Ever since Melanie took over the film and theatre columns, we've had nothing but compliments. Her reviews even get quoted in the movie advertisements."

"And on theatre posters, as well," Melanie added.

His continuous smile took on an oily tinge and his laugh seemed to go on forever. "Yes, she is a treasure," he pronounced and, to prove it, he gave her a hug that also went on far too long. My wife Martha tried to pretend all this was the most normal thing in the world, but the angry flush in her face was a dead giveaway.

"How long have you been working for Wally?" I asked.

"She's been with us since last May. In January, she's coming with me to the International Journalism Conference in Montreal."

Now it was Melanie's turn to explain. "Wally and his wife are separated, and as soon as the divorce papers come through we're going to announce our engagement."

Another announcement! I thought. Hard to know which is the more outrageous.

"She has changed my life," Wally proclaimed proudly.

"So I see. And I expect you've changed hers even more." I heard the edge in my voice and so it was no surprise when Francie came bustling over to the rescue.

"Dad, I want you to meet Warren's classmates from his Russian seminar."

The first was a tall, thin creature — Wilma Something-Or-Other, who instantly became a blur in my mind. But the other gal certainly made her presence felt. Oh, yes! Her name was Natasha Shevchenko and she and her family had arrived in Winnipeg from Moscow that summer. She was dark-haired and very striking. About nineteen, I would guess, with high cheekbones and a smile that seemed to say, "But, of course — I recognized you at once as a kindred spirit," while a mischievous sparkle flashed in her eyes.

"What do you plan to do after your course is finished?"

"When university is over" — again that smile welcomed me into her circle — "I go to New York."

"Why New York?"

"There is a job with a newspaper."

"Oh, yes . . . " I said, puzzled.

"Yes . . . there is a job for me in the office of *Pravda*. Famous Russian paper."

"Do you think you'll like New York?" asked Francie, who was still keeping a concerned eye on me.

"After one year or maybe two, an opening will be in Paris. French for me is not so difficult as English."

"You speak English very well," Warren protested.

For answer she squeezed his arm and smiled that strangely proprietorial smile of hers.

Now what the hell is that supposed to be? I puzzled. Russian camaraderie? Or just plain, old-fashioned flirting?

"Do you find the classroom discussions interesting?" Now I sounded like a university professor.

She nodded enthusiastically, and then, looking at Warren, "Especially I like the translations of Pushkin."

While I was puzzling what to make of this latest disclosure, Francie came rushing over with two other guests.

"Dad, you remember Jackie?"

I looked again and there was Francie's childhood friend, all grown up now: a blonde, wearing a shimmering light-blue blazer and navy slacks and a thin silver hoop threaded through her nose. For a moment, as she greeted me, she moved with the grace of a ballet dancer. Then the moment passed. I recalled that she and Francie had taken ballet lessons together. Still, what I saw before me now bore very little resemblance to the snapshot in my memory book.

"And this is Jackie's friend, Colin." The boy smiled somewhat uneasily, I thought, and then shook my hand.

Jackie fixed him with a brief impatient glance. "Would you bring me a glass of wine?" Her "Please" sounded like an afterthought.

Wordlessly he rushed off to the kitchen.

"Jackie and Colin have been having a tiff," Francie explained.

"Not too serious, I hope."

"More serious than he wants it to be," Jackie replied. "That's the trouble."

"Oh," I responded idiotically, and fled toward the back door just as Colin returned. I needed some fresh air. Or was it a smoke? At any rate, I could do with a few minutes by myself. But when I got to the back hallway, off the kitchen, there in the darkness I could just make out two figures. I was about to edge by them with an "Excuse me" when I realized they were in an embrace and oblivious of everything else.

His hands moved slowly, exploratively, further downward, stroking the curves of her buttocks, then rose along her sides, reached up to her breasts — at which point she flung her head back — eyes closed — before kissing that smiling, middle-aged face passionately on the mouth. It was Melanie. I felt the outrage of a parent whose sense of the rightness of things is being constantly rejected by the world.

Now I was blundering back through the kitchen toward the front door. "Darling, what's the rush?" Martha called out to me. "Isn't Francie handling everything well? I'm just surprised how marvellously she manages: the turkey's about ready to come out of the oven, everyone's got a drink. Not a slip-up that I can see."

I looked into that trusting, gentle face which mirrored Francie's features so clearly.

"Is anything the matter? You look flustered."

"Need a cigarette. Be back in a minute."

"Oh, Peter, you'll spoil your appetite. Besides, I thought you were cutting down."

"Not now, Martha. Not at this precise moment!" And I rushed off.

The cigarette was calming and the cold fresh air felt so good I was tempted to take a stroll around the block, but after a few steps I heard a voice calling out.

"Peter, come back. Where do you think you're going without a coat and hat? We're almost ready to eat, and you're needed to do the carving."

I came back into the house reluctantly. Another drink was what I needed. As I moved toward the kitchen, I was aware of Jackie whispering with Colin in the doorway.

"Doesn't she see he's just taking advantage of her?"

"She doesn't *want* to see."

The voices fell silent as I came over to the liquor table.

"Now, Dad, why don't you hold off on the liquor?" Francie's voice called. "Warren's about to pour everyone a glass of wine."

"Well," I laughed — though in fact I did feel somewhat disconcerted — "I sure do get badgered around here.

Your mother gets after me for having a smoke on the front steps and now you won't let me have a drink."

"But, Dad, we need you to carve the turkey and that will take a steady hand. Mom and you are to sit together at the head of the table."

"Bring out that turkey, then, and let's get on with it."

After everyone had gathered around the table, a few of the guests looked toward me expectantly. Dammit! Must think I'll insist on saying grace. But I'd sure settle for a drink instead. I took a deep breath. "Ready?" I asked the assembled company. "On your mark. Get set. Go!" There was a nervous laugh of relief before everyone began with the soup and I got to work carving up the turkey. The whole table was bright with coloured Russian wine glasses, cut-glass serving plates, polished Swedish cutlery and a couple of bottles of bubbling rosé wine. I looked toward the other end of the table where Warren and Francie sat, and she smiled back at me. She had always been in danger of becoming one of the more lonely kids on the block, but now I could see that life was going to treat her pretty well — and for the duration!

To my left, though, I was aware of Melanie and Wally. She was shaking her head while Wally was whispering something in her ear. Her face reddening, Melanie shifted in her chair. Who knows what's going on under the table? I thought. Then with a laugh and a shrug of his shoulders, he reached for the rosé and proceeded to fill both their glasses to the rim.

Across from them, Jackie and Colin could have been a million miles apart. Colin sat silent, white-faced, and miserable, while Jackie simply looked embarrassed. Desperately she tried to engage Francie — to her right — in conversation. Her movements and gestures had taken on a brusqueness that seemed remote from those of the happy little kid that had grown up in our neighbourhood and then gone on to take ballet.

"Have you met many people since coming to Winnipeg?" I asked Natasha.

"Am I lonely? do you ask?"

"Have you made many friends?"

"Everywhere I meet people. They are — how do you say? — too kind."

"Too kind? What do you mean?"

For answer, Natasha laughed. "I am not helpless. People always are trying everything to do for me."

And I could see why. Her lack of familiarity with life in Canada couldn't help but evoke an immediate offer of help from anyone. And then there was that smile — it would at once place a seal of friendship upon any new encounter.

When the serving plate with the turkey reached Colin, he was left holding it while Jackie continued her conversation with Francie. He tried to win her attention with a timid "Jackie," but she remained oblivious. Finally, it was Francie who drew Jackie's attention to the plate of food.

"Well, for goodness' sake, Colin," she said impatiently, "why didn't you say something?" And before he could reply, she had served herself some turkey and was chatting again to Francie. Nothing to really get upset about, I told myself. But another thought — that I might be seeing the first hint of something else — kept trying to insinuate itself, unsettling and unnerving, into my consciousness. There was something altogether too brusque and mannish about Jackie's manner to suit me. And hadn't

I heard from Francie that Jackie would soon be moving into an apartment with a girlfriend? So why does that seem so alarming? And then — unsummoned — the answer flitted darkly through my mind. I looked across the table to Francie again to see her reaction, but she was now chatting to Wilma What's-Her-Name.

Just as well, I thought.

"It does me good to see her like this," Martha whispered, reading my mind. "She was such a shy child."

In response, I lifted my glass to Francie in a silent toast. Whatever was up with her two girlfriends, she was well out of it. Later during the meal, in the midst of the chatter, I could just make out a whispered voice saying, "Yes, it's all very well now, but she may be sorry later." Quickly I looked up to see if Melanie had heard, but she had other matters on her mind just then. Enjoy what you can, I lectured myself. People have their own lives to lead. In a few months Francie would be having her baby and a month after that Warren would be writing civil service exams for a position with Foreign Affairs. Those prospects I could look forward to. And so we stayed on during the evening, even though Martha would have preferred to leave Francie and Warren alone with their guests. But frankly I couldn't face up to those Hindu chants droning through the house. So I had one Scotch and then another and then Martha insisted I have some coffee before we set off in the car.

By then the evening was breaking up and Francie asked if I'd drop Wilma off on the way home. "It's not much out of your way," she explained. "She lives in Fort Richmond."

It was while we were all locating our coats that I heard Melanie whispering to Wally: "That kind of behaviour is really intolerable. And she's been like that all evening." I looked about, but Colin and Jackie must have left only moments before. Clearly Jackie's coldness to Colin had not gone unnoticed and Francie's guests had lost all sympathy.

"I think she's outrageous."

"Well, one thing's certain. *That* situation can't go on."

"You're telling me!"

Just when we were almost ready to depart, Wilma couldn't locate her purse, so we stood around waiting in the warmth of the hallway for a few moments more while she looked for it. The conversation drifted into talk about assignments that were due and the last few papers that had been delivered in class.

"I thought Wilma's report last week — it did not really deal with the issues — what is really central to Pushkin. Do you not agree?"

"But there was no other way to deal with the topic. You must see that." Warren's opinion was instantly accepted.

"Yes, of course. I had not thought of that," Natasha conceded. Then, after a pause, in a teasing voice: "Oh, oh, I am so . . . terrified . . . of your intellect."

There was a burst of laughter among the group just as Wilma appeared at last with her purse. Then there was a buttoning up of coats as we edged toward the door.

"No, no, it is alright," Natasha was saying to Francie. "I will phone for a cab."

"Sorry," I said. "I hadn't realized you didn't have a ride." And then seeing her look up — surprised — I added, "Come along with us."

"No . . . no . . . it is out of your way. Miles and miles. In Transcona."

There was a momentary silence within the group.

"Can't you go along with Melanie and Wally?" Francie asked.

"They've just left," a voice replied.

Natasha was looking in the yellow pages for a cab.

"It'll cost the earth," I said. Though I knew that driving to Transcona and back would take close to an hour, some instinct made me repeat the offer.

"No, no, it is too far," Natasha insisted.

"Oh, Dad," Francie said, "I can't let you turn into my own personal taxi service. Warren, will you drive Natasha home?"

"Of course."

"But you don't mind?" Again that smile drew them all to her.

"It's all arranged then. Hold on, Natasha, and I'll get my coat."

In the car, Martha, Wilma and I settled down into a muffled silence. "Don't race," I warned myself as we approached the corner. Once Wilma had been let off in Fort Richmond, there was nothing for it but to drive home and see what welcomed us there. And sure enough, as soon as we entered the door, I could hear Bobby chanting at the Hindu shrine downstairs.

"God, doesn't he ever let up?" I blurted out.

"It's just a phase, Peter. Don't blow it up out of all proportion. Next year, it will be Tai Chi, and you'll be complaining about that."

"I can hardly wait."

So we went to bed and soon all the good food and wine began to do their work and I kept drifting in and out of sleep — forever, it seemed. From below, the faint buzz and hum of Bobby's chanting reached up to the bedroom, but the room itself was filled with dreams of a lavish dinner, of our daughter soon to have a baby of her own, of Warren writing those civil service exams. And if all goes well: Foreign Affairs. Warren the Traveller. Yes, he would be good at that. He was a traveller. Driving that classmate of his home. What was her name? Natasha. The Hindu chants had long ceased when the urgent ringing of the phone finally woke me from my dreams.

"Hi, Dad?"

"Francie?"

"Yes."

"My God, it can't be morning already."

Beside me, Martha had stirred into wakefulness and was gazing at me with a strained look.

"Is there anything wrong, Francie?"

"I'm not sure. Warren isn't over there, is he?"

"Warren? No. Should he be?"

"Has Warren had an accident?" Martha whispered urgently.

"Stop it, Martha. Everything's fine. Just fine." But what I asked Francie next indicated otherwise. "Why would Warren be here?"

There was a pause that lasted so long I thought we'd been cut off before she answered, "I don't know. Thought maybe he'd wanted to talk to you."

With a start I recalled that Warren and I hadn't exchanged more than a word or two all evening. "No, he's not here," I repeated carefully. "Maybe his car broke down."

"But wouldn't he have phoned? I've already called all the main hospitals. And the police."

And then I realized why I had felt such a sense of unease throughout the evening. At first, I had put it down to Melanie's situation. And to Jackie's strangeness. But it seems I had missed the point of all that whispering — perhaps it hadn't been just Melanie and Jackie that were being talked about.

It's all very well now, but she may be sorry later.
I think she's outrageous.
Well, one thing's certain. That situation can't go on.

"How long ago is it, Francie, since we left your place?"

"Hours ago. It's past four in the morning, Dad, and the party broke up around midnight. Surely he would have phoned by now if . . . "

"And you've already called the hospitals? And the police?"

"Dad, I've already told you."

"Well, I guess that just leaves one last call to make."

"Yes."

"Ring me back right away."

While waiting for her to call, I explained to Martha what she had already guessed. She was silent for a moment, then said simply, "I'll get some tea." But ten minutes later she still hadn't returned from the kitchen. I expected she was drawing back into herself as she agonized over the situation.

Still feeling puzzled, I sat on the edge of the bed and stared at the floor as I reviewed all the events of the evening in the light of what Francie had just told me. What I ended up with left me feeling dazed. When the phone did at last ring, I caught it up at once.

"You were right."

"But what did he say?"

"She was the one answered the phone. And what she said was, 'Well, it's not my fault. Warren, he can make his own decisions. He is not — you know — a baby.'"

"And what did you say?"

"I just got too mad listening to that blundering, awkward voice."

"So?"

"So I said what was true: 'That's where you're wrong — he is a baby, a great big baby!'"

"Do you know what I think?"

"What?"

"Well, I too am terrified of his intellect."

Despite herself, she laughed.

"And I agree. He is a baby."

"It's not going to do any good calling him names, Dad. He's my husband . . . and . . . " Uncertainly, her voice subsided into silence.

"Look, I'll come over right away."

"You don't have to, Dad. I'll be alright."

"Be there in fifteen minutes."

Quickly I got dressed, and as I was leaving the room the card that I had left on top of the dresser caught my eye. There was the photo of Cindy, in her red negligée, staring so intently at the baby. I studied the wedding announcement. Had it arrived just a few days ago? It seemed like another age. Like the declaration of a new dispensation.

As I left the house, I was aware of its silence. I listened caarefully, but there was not a sound. For a moment, I was tempted to flee to the downstairs bedroom, wake Bobby from his sleep and chant with him for the rest of the night at his makeshift shrine.

But in front of me the cold, deserted streets, soon to be ice-locked for the entire winter, beckoned me on.

Printed in September 1998 by
VEILLEUX ON DEMAND PRINTING INC.
in Boucherville, Quebec